Lea
Dives
In

by Lisa Yee

★ American Girl®

For Jodi, Dan, and Sara

Published by American Girl Publishing

16 17 18 19 20 21 22 23 24 LEO 12 11 10 9 8 7 6 5 4 3 2

All American Girl marks, Lea™, Lea Clark™, and Girl of the Year™ are trademarks of American Girl.

This book is a work of fiction. Any similarity to real persons, living or dead, is coincidental and not intended by American Girl. References to real events, people, or places are used fictitiously. Other names, characters, places, and incidents are the products of imagination.

Illustrations by Sarah Davis

Author photo credit, p. 152: Mieke Kramer

Special thanks to Julie Kline, founder of the Américas Award for Children's and Young Adult Literature; and Nola Senna, Director, Undergraduate Portuguese Language and Brazilian Studies, University of Illinois at Urbana-Champaign.

americangirl.com/service

Contents

The Adventure Begins
Chapter 1

L ea, don't forget your camera," Dad yelled from the hallway.

My camera! I sure didn't want to leave that behind. I couldn't wait to start taking pictures of my first big adventure outside of St. Louis. I realized that I was a little nervous—I had never even been outside of Missouri before, yet in twenty-four hours I would be 4,500 miles away in Brazil—and I didn't know a word of Portuguese! But with a camera in my hands, I felt like I could go anywhere without looking out of place.

Ever since I got my brother's hand-me-down camera when I was six, I've loved taking photos. And when my grandmother gave me a new camera for my tenth birthday, I took it with me everywhere I went. Last year I won third place in a national

1

kids' magazine contest for my photo collage of St. Louis. I couldn't wait to start taking photos in Brazil! Would I capture the shot that would win me first place?

I've decided to be a photographer when I grow up. Well, that or a veterinarian, or maybe a travel writer, or a paramedic, or ... something else entirely. My grandmother always said, "Lea, you should be open to trying new things. Life is like a buffet to be sampled!"

I picked up my camera and stared at my overstuffed suitcase. I had no clue how I was going to pack everything I wanted to. After all, I needed room for the necessities, such as my sea turtle identification book, my passport with its butterfly cover, a photo of my turtle Ginger, and of course my new bathing suit. I felt a rush of excitement as I imagined the sun warming my face and shoulders on the Brazilian beach. It was freezing in late January in St. Louis, Missouri, and outside my window in Lafayette Square I could see the clapboard houses dusted with snow. But we were heading south of the equator, where it was summer!

The Adventure Begins

"Ahem!" Dad shook me out of my daydream. "How do I look?"

He was standing in the doorway wearing clunky hiking boots, pants with too many pockets, a complicated fishing vest, and a green cloth hat with long flaps on three sides that covered his short, dark brown hair. Everything still had the price tags on. I cringed when I imagined Dad walking around Brazil wearing this ridiculous outfit. Was he really going to wear all that—at once?

"What?" my father asked when he saw the horror on my face. "If we're tromping through the Amazon rainforest, I want to be prepared." He tried to yank one of the price tags off. "Don't you think Zac will be impressed?"

"You can't . . ." I stopped when I saw him laughing, and then feigned seriousness and said, "Yes, Dad, Zac's going to be totally impressed."

Thinking about Zac made me smile. I hadn't seen my big brother in ages, and he was the reason we were going to Brazil.

Zac and I spent a lot of time together when I was little, especially when Mom and Dad had

to work late, which was quite often. I used to follow him like a shadow and we'd talk nonstop—me asking him questions, him giving me the answers. Zac even nicknamed me "Cricket" because he said I was always "chirping up."

But after Zac left for college in California three years ago, the house grew quiet—and so did I. I missed him so much that sometimes I'd hang out in his bedroom and pretend that he was just in another room. Then when Zac headed to Brazil for a year to study the rainforests, that meant not even seeing him at Christmas.

My father stepped over my clothes strewn across the floor and gave me a hug. "It's going to be great with all of us being together again," he said, adding, "I miss him, too."

After Dad left, I sat on my bed and stared at my suitcase. The dark brown leather was battered and looked as if it was held together with stickers from all over the world. It had belonged to Ama, my grandmother.

Ama was my hero. She smelled like orange blossoms, and could roar like a lion, and was the

bravest person I had ever known. Who else had
a grandmother who climbed mountains, and boogie-
boarded in the ocean, and made friends in every
country she visited?

The last time I saw Ama, she was in the hospital.
Though she struggled to sit up in bed, her familiar
smile came easily. The sun was setting, and the room
was bathed in a golden glow. She motioned me to her
and slowly unclasped the small compass necklace
that she always wore.

"Lean forward, Lea," she said. When I did,
she put it around my neck. "This compass has been
my travel companion for years—even before I was a
world traveler." Ama's voice was weak. I moved closer.
"It has pointed me toward all kinds of adventures,
and now it can accompany you on yours."

I lifted the pendant to the light and admired the
red flower design on the face of the compass. "Thank
you, Ama," I said.

She nodded, and pulled me in to a tight hug.
A nurse came in and said that it was time for Ama
to rest. That night, while I was sleeping, my grandmother passed away peacefully.

I picked up the compass from my dresser and fastened the cord around my neck. Would this compass help me in Brazil?

Mom appeared in my doorway. She was carrying some old books with an orange ribbon wrapped around them.

"Join me for a second," she said, sitting down on my bed.

I sat next to her and peered at the mysterious books as she placed them in my lap.

"Ama wanted you to have these," my mother said. "She told me to give them to you when the time was right."

"What are they?" I asked.

"Her travel journals," Mom explained. "Ama wrote about all of her world adventures in these."

I looked down at the journals. They were simply numbered One, Two, Three, Four. Each had a worn cover of soft red leather.

"Did you read them?" I asked. I ran my fingertips across the first book's cover.

My mother nodded. "She led quite a life. Some people don't like to try new things as they get older.

Your grandmother wasn't like that. In fact, she got *more* adventurous with age."

"You mean she wasn't always a world traveler?" I asked.

Mom shook her head. "When I was your age, she always stayed close to home. Ama was busy working, and driving me places, and always volunteering at my school. I never thought of her as someone who would one day climb mountains and go on dinosaur fossil digs. Later, though, it didn't surprise me. When I think back, I realize she always had that spark."

"Like Zac," I said.

"Hmm . . . yes, I suppose so," Mom agreed. "And I see that spark in you, too, Lea."

I felt my cheeks go warm and touched the compass pendant that hung around my neck. Would I ever be a world traveler like my grandmother had been? I had always wanted to be.

Once when I was in kindergarten, I announced, "When I grow up I want to be just like you, Ama!"

"That's funny," she said. Her hazel eyes sparkled mischievously. "Because I want to be just like *you*!"

And so you know what Ama did? She put her

gray hair into two braids that matched mine! Even though I eventually outgrew that hairstyle, my grandmother never did.

I looked down at her travel journals. The covers were battered, and many of the pages were wavy, as if they had gotten wet and then dried all crinkly. I could hardly wait to read about Ama's journeys all over the world. As I embarked on my own journey, it would be almost like taking her with me.

A Familiar Face

Chapter 2

As I looked out the airplane window, I could see mountains below. They looked so small that they reminded me of the relief map of Missouri that my best friend Abby and I had once made for school. Mom had told me that I should try to get some sleep since our journey would take over sixteen hours, but I was too excited to sleep. I was going to see Zac!

Zac and I both love animals. Ama was always sending photos of herself doing things like swimming with dolphins, riding a camel, or even holding a huge snake. We lived for her photos and wanted to *be* her! I wondered what wild animals I'd see in the rainforest. A jaguar, maybe? Caimans, of course. Toucans and snakes, I hoped. And monkeys, lots and lots of monkeys! But first, we were going to stay at the beach, which was about fifteen hundred miles

away from the Amazon. This would be a first for me—seeing the ocean—and I couldn't wait.

While Mom and Dad slept, I pulled the stack of Ama's journals out of my backpack, untied the ribbon, and opened the first one. It was stuffed with photos and airplane ticket stubs and other scraps of paper, like phone numbers of people she had met. Pasted into the inside cover was a worn black-and-white wedding photo of a young man and woman looking deliriously happy. I looked closely. The bride was Ama! I'd recognize her smile anywhere. The groom was Grandpa Bill. He died long before I was born, but Mom and Ama had told me so many stories about him that I felt as if I knew him.

I turned to the first page of the journal. In Ama's familiar loopy handwriting it began:

I have decided to stop making excuses and to start traveling like Bill and I always wanted to. I'm a little nervous about traveling alone, but if I don't start now, when will I? Hello world, Amanda Cooper is coming your way!

A Familiar Face

I turned the page, eager to find out where Ama had traveled to first.

Aloha from Hawaii! she wrote. *Even though I'm in the United States, I feel as if I'm in another country. The island of Kauai is so beautiful—and the beaches, ah, the beaches. I'm definitely not in St. Louis anymore. Today when I was snorkeling, a giant sea turtle swam past me. At first I panicked—he was huge! But then I realized I wasn't that interesting to him, and he just kept going. Neither one of us was in a hurry, and I marveled at the sight of him. I've read that sea turtles bring good luck, so judging by the size of this one, I'll have good fortune for many years to come!*

To think I was once scared of traveling alone and now I can't wait to figure out where I'll go next. Paris? Greece? The Galapagos Islands? Ah, but before I decide, it's time to hit the waves . . . after all, I won't see anything exciting from the inside of a hotel room! Now that I've gone to the trouble of traveling to a new place, I should see and do everything I can.

Lea Dives In

Gotta go—time for my windsurfing lesson!

On the next page was a photo of Ama standing next to a windsurfing board on the Hawaiian beach. Her wavy brown hair was streaked with gray and was worn loose, skimming her shoulders. Ama's high cheekbones and freckles reminded me of my mother, and people often said that we shared the same big hazel eyes. But Ama's slightly crooked, totally radiant smile was all her own.

The date in the journal was 1996—twenty years ago. My brother would have been just a few months old.

When Zac announced that he wanted to study the Amazon rainforest, no one was surprised. In college he was an environmental studies major. Like Ama, he craved adventure. Despite my parents' initial objections, for his twentieth birthday, my grandmother took Zac skydiving. I have a photo of the two of them in the air, grinning.

It was Ama who had convinced my parents to let Zac study in the Amazon rainforest. "My father came to the United States from Brazil when he was a boy," she began. "That means Zac is one-eighth Brazilian. So it only seems right that we send our young man from the United States back to South America, even if it is just for a year!"

My mother thought it would be dangerous. My father thought it would be expensive. But with Ama on his side, Zac couldn't lose. She had a way of getting people to do things her way, by making it seem like it was their idea.

"He needs to test himself," she argued. "He's ready."

"Zac can test himself right here in the United States," Dad said.

"There are wild animals in the rainforest," Mom pointed out. "And poisonous plants, and—"

"And with any luck he will see them," Ama noted.

"He could catch malaria," said Mom.

"He'll get medicine before he goes," Ama assured her.

The arguments went back and forth like a doubles tennis match, and in the end, the team of Ama and Zac triumphed.

"Well, it is a wonderful chance to broaden your horizons, Zac," Dad said. "I wish I had studied abroad when I was in college."

"And Ama does have a good point about living with a family in the Brazilian rainforest being a once-in-a-lifetime opportunity," Mom mused. "What an experience that will be!"

And away Zac went, just like that.

No one had asked for my opinion.

It was after midnight when we landed in Salvador, Brazil. Soon we would be meeting Zac at the hotel! I watched the suitcases going around and around the luggage carousel. They were mostly black, including ours—but Mom had tied big red ribbons around the handles so that we could spot them easily. It was a trick she had learned from Ama.

As my parents struggled with the luggage, I glanced around the airport. Near the doors were a few men, each holding a sign with a name on it. These were drivers who were hired to take visitors to their hotels. Chan Family, DiNovas, Dr. Birdsall . . .

# A Familiar Face

Família Clark. That was us!

It was hard to see the driver because the sign was covering his face. Plus, I was sleepy. However, when I heard him yell "Cricket!" I snapped awake. There was only one person in the world who called me that.

"It's you!" I screamed, running toward him.

"Lea!" Mom called out. "What are you doing?" She paused, then cried out, "Zac!"

"Zac?" Dad said, spinning around. "Zac!"

I was the first to get to him.

"Cricket!" he laughed as I leaped into his arms. He tried to spin me around in the air the way we used to do when I was little—and we both almost fell over.

Mom and Dad joined us for what I am fairly certain was the longest group hug in the history of Brazil.

We hadn't expected to see Zac at the airport. And he didn't even look like Zac. His short brown hair was now longish and wavy and had flecks of blond, and his tanned face was covered with stubble. He just barely resembled the pale, skinny goofball I remembered. This new Zac was sort of rugged and

more athletic looking. However, his blue eyes still had
that sparkle that told me this was my big brother. He
mussed up my hair, and I grinned back at him.

"Let me look at you, Cricket," Zac said, taking a
step back. "Hmm, your eyes are still hazel, and your
hair is still light brown, but it's longer than I remembered. Still, I'd recognize that crazy smile anywhere.
You've grown!"

It was true. Recently I'd had a growth spurt, and
I was nearly two inches taller than the last time Zac
had seen me at the end of the summer. I was now tall
enough to hook arms with him as we left the airport.

By the time we finally checked into the hotel,
I was exhausted. I could hear the waves, but even
with the moon out it was hard to see them. I could
barely keep my eyes open. "Can we go to the beach
now?" I asked drowsily.

"It'll still be there in the morning," Mom
assured me.

"But I can't wait . . . " I began. "I came all this
way, and if I don't see the ocean, then I'll . . . I'll . . . "

Before I could even finish my sentence, I was
asleep.

Making a Splash
Chapter 3

It was dark when I woke. For a moment I forgot where I was. Startled, I bolted upright and looked around. That's when I remembered. I wasn't in St. Louis, Missouri, anymore. I was in Salvador, Brazil—and the sound I was hearing was the ocean waves!

I jumped out of bed and almost tripped over the luggage before pulling back the curtains. The bright sunlight blinded me at first, but when my eyes adjusted I gasped. A thin strip of golden sand lay between a rocky sea wall and water shimmering in a shade of turquoise blue I never even knew existed.

I knelt and rooted around my suitcase, tossing my homework assignments aside until I found what I was looking for. When I stepped out on the balcony,

I immediately began to take photos with the camera Ama had given me.

I had been waiting for this moment for so long. Practically all my friends had been to the ocean. My best friend Abby had been to the beach THREE times—twice in Florida and once in California.

"You're going to love, love, love the beach!" Abby had declared. We were catching the after-Christmas sales at Chloe's Closet, the only store in Lafayette Square that sells bathing suits year-round. "Here, try these on," she said, piling a half dozen swimsuits into my arms. "And come out after you put them on, so I can see each one!"

My family was still asleep when I changed into my Abby-approved bathing suit. I was so excited that I put both legs into one side. When I fell over, Mom and Zac slept through it, though Dad mumbled, "I already took out the trash."

As my family continued to doze, I said softly, "Time to wake up."

No one did.

I cleared my throat. "Excuse me? Time to go to the beach," I said, louder.

Dad rolled over and Mom put her arm across her eyes.

Zac didn't even move, but then he was always a solid sleeper.

"Let's go swimming!" I shouted.

When my parents groaned and insisted they needed coffee first, I turned to Zac, who was barely awake. "Please, go with me to the beach," I begged.

"Just ten more minutes, Cricket," he mumbled. "Let me sleep ten more minutes."

"Zac," Dad said, his eyes still closed, "please take your sister to the beach."

"Go with Lea," Mom said, sounding muffled. It was a miracle that we could hear her at all since she was facedown in her pillow. "And be sure not to let her out of your sight, especially in the water."

My brother had never been a morning person, and this, at least, hadn't changed. As we crossed the street leading to the beach, he looked like a zombie. "This is my vacation, too, Cricket," he grumbled. "I wanted to sleep in."

I waved him off. I was too happy feeling the warm sand under my feet and noticing that the

waves lapping the shore looked like the white peaks on the top of a lemon meringue pie.

This was the moment I had dreamed about. I took a step forward and let the waves lap my feet. I stopped and closed my eyes to smell the salty sea air. It was like a perfume, and it wrapped around me like a hug.

My heart swelling with anticipation, I looked out at the ocean and took a big step forward. My pulse was racing. At first I thought it was because I was so excited to see the ocean. But all at once, I realized that I was scared.

A memory flashed in my mind. I must have been only about six years old, but it felt as if it were yesterday. I was sitting on the dock at Mark Twain State Park, dipping my toes in the water, when I leaned down to look at my reflection—and fell face-first into the lake. I flailed around in a panic. The dock was too high above the water for my short arms to reach. I knew how to swim—I had reached level three in swimming lessons—but as I tried to swim toward a ladder a few feet away, my head went under and I accidentally inhaled water through my nose. I couldn't breathe, I couldn't shout for help, I couldn't even cry. I had never been so terrified in my life.

I was probably underwater only a few seconds, but it felt like a lifetime. Luckily, Zac had seen me. He jumped in and pulled me to safety, and before long I was in Ama's comforting arms.

"I was so scared," I confessed to Ama. She had been eager to take us to the park, and I wondered if I had let her down. "I'm not like you," I told her sadly. "You're always so brave."

My grandmother held me tighter. "Oh, Lea," she said, "I'm not fearless, but I don't let my fear stop me from doing the things I really want to do. You'll swim again," she assured me.

Ama was right, of course. For the next few summers I continued taking lessons at our local pool. I always tried to avoid putting my head underwater—and I never did try swimming in a lake again. But this was bigger than any lake—this was the Atlantic Ocean. And it had *waves.*

I shuddered at the memory and looked out toward the ocean. Then I remembered what Ama wrote

in her journal: *Now that I've gone to the trouble of travel-ing to a new place, I should see and do everything I can.*

Well, I was *seeing* the ocean. That was step one. So far, so good. But if Ama was right, I should do more than just look at it. After all, I could do *that* from my hotel room—and Ama's point was to get out there and *do* stuff.

I took a deep breath. Today was the day I was going to swim in the Atlantic Ocean!

The sand and water tickled my toes as the waves rolled in to the shore. Some were slow, others fast, thinning out by the time they got to me. I took an-other step. My feet sank until they were covered with soft, wet sand, and it was hard to lift them. Was this what quicksand was like? I took another step and then another until the water was up to my knees. So far, so good ...

Zac ran past me, splashing and then diving into the water. When he surfaced, he waded back toward me with a mischievous grin and shouted, "Cricket, watch out, there's a wave coming at you!"

I looked around, but could see no waves on the horizon. Then, without warning, Zac pushed

a big splash of water at me.

"Surf's up!" he called, laughing.

I opened my mouth to tell him to stop and got a huge mouthful of seawater. I began to choke and spit out the water. It was salty! Duh—*of course*, the ocean would be salty, but I hadn't really planned on drinking it.

"Zac!" I screamed as he continued to splash me and laugh. "Stop it! It's not funny—stop it!"

"Chill, Cricket," he said, looking disappointed. "It's no big deal, it's just water."

But it wasn't just water. It was salty, and it was in my nose and my eyes. The more I rubbed my eyes, the more irritated they became.

"That wasn't very nice," I told him.

"Oh, come on," he said. "Don't tell me you're upset over a little water?"

Just then I saw my parents coming toward us. "So, Lea, how do you like your first swim in the ocean?" Mom called as she stepped into the water. Her short, sandy brown hair and the spray of freckles marching across her nose made her look years younger than she really was.

I shrugged. I didn't want anyone to know how upset I was.

"Lea? Is everything okay?" Mom asked. She turned to Zac. He just shrugged.

"I'm fine," I muttered through gritted teeth. Mom frowned, concerned. I let go of a sigh. "Really, I'm fine," I assured her. The last thing I wanted to do was ruin everyone's vacation.

"I'm just going to take a break," I announced. There was sand in my mouth and it crunched between my teeth when I spoke.

"Hey, Cricket?" Zac called after me.

I ignored him and headed to a beach chair, plopped myself down, and crossed my arms.

From the shore I could see my parents splashing in the water, acting like kids. Dad picked up Mom and whirled her around while she splashed him. He didn't seem to mind getting water in his face.

My eyes still stung from the salt water, and I squeezed them shut. Then I sensed something blocking my sun. I squinted and saw Zac standing above me.

"What's up, Cricket?" he asked. "You're not mad

at me, are you? I'm sorry if I got you upset."

"I'm not upset," I lied.

"Good!" he said. Smiling, Zac shook his head like a dog and showered me with water coming off his hair. Though he might have thought this was funny, I certainly didn't. "How do you like the beach?"

I wanted to say, *You try choking on salt water and getting it in your eyes and nose, and see how* you *like it.*

"It's amazing," I said. And it was—amazing to *look* at.

"Isn't it?" Zac said, shading his eyes. "I wish we could stay longer, but Dad says we need to check out of the hotel soon."

"Aw, too bad," I said, secretly relieved.

"Don't worry," Zac assured me. "If you like this beach, you're going to *love* Praia Tropical. It's one of the most beautiful beaches in Bahia."

Great. Another beach where I can make a fool of myself.

"And get this," Zac continued. "There's a big sea turtle sanctuary nearby."

I perked up. "Turtles?"

25

"Hey, that reminds me," Zac said. "How's old Ginger?"

"Ginger's good," I said, thinking fondly of my own little turtle back home. "Abby's babysitting her." I hoped I had left enough dried shrimp for Ginger's daily treat. "It was so funny—last week Ginger climbed between her two rocks and it looked like she got stuck, but—"

"That's nice," Zac said. He was looking at a sailboat on the horizon.

"So, is the Amazon rainforest very far from here?" I asked, changing the subject. Clearly, my Ginger story had bored him. Maybe I could convince my parents to cut down our beach time and go to the rainforest sooner! I was eager to see the wild animals—and not too eager to swallow any more salt water.

Zac turned to me and raised his eyebrows in a way that made me wonder whether I had asked a dumb question. "Well, yeah, the Amazon rainforest is practically on the other side of the country," he said, as if this was something everyone knew. Well, everyone but me. "Brazil is huge—larger than the

26

United States, not counting Alaska. Right now we're in Bahia, one of twenty-six states here in Brazil. It's famous for soccer, and seafood, and ... "

As my brother rambled on, I felt like I was back in school listening to someone's geography report. My eyes began to glaze over as Zac continued to lecture me. "Okay, okay! I get it," I interrupted, annoyed. "The Amazon rainforest is far away."

Zac's mouth snapped shut and he nodded. "Fine. Just trying to be helpful," he said curtly. "You asked me a question, remember?"

For an awkward moment we just looked at each other, and neither of us had anything to say.

Something about Zac was different. Every time Ama used to come home from a trip she'd joke that Zac and I had grown so much she hardly recognized us. But this time, it wasn't just that my brother *looked* different. He *acted* different, too.

And now I realized that I didn't even know how to talk to him.

Three Wishes

Chapter 4

Before we left for Praia Tropical, Mom and Dad took us to visit Pelourinho, Salvador's historic district. In the more modern area of the city near our hotel, the streets had been paved and the buildings were clean and new. But here in Pelourinho, I felt as if I had stepped out of a time machine. Old stone churches towered up toward the clear blue sky. Inside, some even glistened with gold. Real gilt paint and gold leaf! I took lots of photos to show Abby.

My mother is an architect who restores historic buildings, and as we walked, she pointed out the different kinds of architecture and explained what the buildings were made of. Dad's a history professor at Washington University in St. Louis, so whenever there was a plaque on a building or it was featured

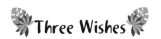

in his guidebook, he'd get all excited.

Each of the colonial buildings that lined both sides of the gray stone streets was drenched in bright colors—green, yellow, blue, red, orange—and the way the colored roofs and gables slanted up, one on top of another, reminded me of an open box of crayons. As we maneuvered down the narrow sidewalks, Dad tried to walk and read his guidebook at the same time, and he would have fallen twice had Mom not been there to steer him.

Dad pointed to the page that he was reading and said, "It says here that much of the food, music, and culture around us was influenced by African heritage that goes back centuries."

I trained my camera on a group of dark-skinned women who all wore white, layered dresses with frilly sleeves, white headscarves, and colorful beaded necklaces. They stood behind tables that held several trays of delicious-looking snacks. One woman carried a handful of rainbow-colored ribbons. Was there a festival going on? I was about to ask Dad if it said anything in his guidebook about some sort of event when I heard a rumbling in the distance.

"What's that sound?" I asked Zac.

"Drums. Wherever you are in Salvador, you can hear them," Zac answered. "To the Brazilian people, music is like air. It's just a natural part of life." He playfully drummed on the top of my head.

When I was younger I would have loved this. But I wasn't a little girl anymore. I pushed him away.

Across the town square we came across a church with an iron gate guarding the entrance. You had to look closely to see the gate, because every inch of it was covered with colorful ribbons just like those I had seen the woman in white carrying by the handful. I pulled out my camera and took a photo of the ribbons fluttering in the breeze.

"It's beautiful," Mom said with a gasp.

"Are the ribbons for decoration?" I asked.

"Those are wish ribbons," Zac explained. *"Senhor do Bonfim*, the savior of Bahia, grants the wishes of anyone who ties a ribbon around their wrist or something like a church gate."

Wish ribbons? I loved the idea! "Can I get one?" I asked. "I saw a lady in white holding a ton of them!"

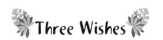

Three Wishes

Zac nodded. As he led us across the square, he explained about the ladies wearing white. "They're called *Baianas,* or women of Bahia. You'll see them all over Salvador, selling traditional Afro Brazilian food and, of course, wish bracelets."

The woman in the white dress greeted us with a big smile and asked me which color I would like. Zac explained that each color has a special meaning. Red was for strength and passion, yellow for success, turquoise for love and peace, pink for friendship, and so on. I selected orange for courage.

Dad dug into his wallet and gave the woman a couple of colorful Brazilian dollar bills, which Zac had told me are called *reals.*

I held out my wrist for Zac to help me tie on the ribbon.

He began knotting it. "*Um, dois, três,*" he counted in Portuguese. "You're supposed to have a friend tie it on using three knots. Then you make a different wish for each knot. Wearing the ribbon reminds you of your wishes, and when it falls off your wishes have been granted."

I closed my eyes and thought of a wish that

I wanted to come true so badly that I wished it three times:

I wish for the courage to swim in the ocean.
I wish for the courage to swim in the ocean.
I wish for the courage to swim in the ocean.

I looked down and admired my bracelet. "What if I just cut it off to get my wish?" I asked.

"That would bring bad luck," Zac said. "The bracelet has to fall off on its own."

"How long will that take?" I asked, examining the ribbon. I really needed it to fall off immediately, because we'd probably visit the beach again when we got to Praia Tropical.

"It could take a while," Zac explained. "A week, a month, maybe several months."

Several months?! We were going to be at the beach all week. There was no way I could wait that long.

Praia Tropical
Chapter 5

The drive from Salvador up the coast was going to take more than three hours, and I was already bored. "So how are you?" I asked Zac as we sped toward Praia Tropical in my parents' rental car.

"Sleepy," he said, stretching his arms.

"I was hoping we could talk," I said as I lowered the window. The warm breeze was soothing. "You know, catch up with each other."

"Okay, sure, Cricket." Zac stifled a yawn. "You start." He slipped his sunglasses on.

There was so much I wanted to tell him—about my teacher Ms. Swain, and my photography, and Ginger, and . . . Zac fell asleep before I could say one word. I didn't have much time to feel insulted, though, because I fell asleep shortly after him.

My brother and I woke up at the same time,

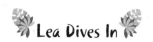

just as we were pulling into *Resort Castelo de Areia,*
which Zac said means "Sand Castle Hotel." As I
gazed at the lush tropical beauty of the beach un-
folding before me, I felt as if I had wandered into a
dream. The golden sand seemed to stretch for miles,
and tall palm trees bowed toward the water. The
sea was a deep, translucent shade of turquoise blue
and looked as if it were lit from below. A rainbow of
worn wooden rowboats rested on the sand with nets
and barnacled cages tossed haphazardly onboard,
while local fishermen laughed and swapped stories
in the shade. I touched my compass necklace. Ama
would have loved it here.

"We'd better hurry if we want to get in some
beach time before the sun sets," Mom said as soon as
we dropped off our suitcases in our room.

Gulp. We hadn't even been here for five minutes
and already my family was ready to hit the waves.
Trying to stall, I slowly opened my suitcase and pretended to dig around for my swimsuit. Then I saw
my camera and had an idea. While the thought of
swimming in the ocean still made me nervous, *looking* at it was something I was happy to do.

"I'll race you to the water," Zac said. "And I promise not to splash you this time."

"Um, no. I need to take some photos."

Zac spun around. "Photos? Now?"

"Yeah," I said. But I could tell he needed a better excuse. "They're for, um . . . a homework assignment," I said weakly.

"Seriously?" Zac snorted. "You're in Brazil. At the beach. On vacation. Come on, Cricket! Your homework can wait—let's swim!"

I bristled. Before Zac went off to college, I was happy to do whatever he wanted to do, and I loved any attention he gave me. But now I wished he'd leave me alone.

I noticed that he had a glob of sunscreen on his face where he hadn't rubbed it all the way in. I didn't tell him about it.

"Zac," I said sweetly, "I know it's summer here and you're on vacation, but back in St. Louis school is in session. Not only do I have to keep up with my homework, but I have to do an extra-credit assignment about Brazil." I picked up a math book, along with Ama's first journal. I was almost halfway

through it, and it was giving me some ideas for my extra-credit assignment. I slipped the books into a light backpack, along with my camera, and followed Zac out the back door of our room and onto a path to the beach.

My parents were walking hand in hand way ahead of us, but my mother did her mom thing where you think she can't hear you, but she can. Teachers have this skill, too.

Mom turned around and gave me a warm smile. "I know we promised Ms. Swain that you'd do all your assignments, but we're also here to have fun, Lea. There will be plenty of time for homework at night."

I nodded and clutched my camera. Maybe I could just take a few photos. After all, with the sun hitting the water, it looked as if someone had tossed a million jewels across the surface of the sea. "I'm going to take some pictures first," I announced. "Abby is going to want to see this!"

My parents shrugged and threw our towels down on some beach chairs before running into the foamy white waves with Zac close behind. Mom and

Zac swam so far out that all I could see were their heads bobbing in the water. Dad stayed closer to shore near me.

Will I ever be brave enough to swim in the ocean? I wondered as I hit the zoom button on my camera to frame a shot of Mom and Zac.

So I got some salt water in my eyes and nose, and sand in my mouth—that's not a big deal, right? Zac once ate dirt when he was little. And that was on purpose.

Maybe I could try it again.

I settled onto a beach chair and opened Ama's journal. Now she was writing about her trip to Norway.

The fjords are so beautiful, but the water is arctic! This morning, they served us pickled herring for breakfast, which seemed a bit odd but was actually quite delicious.

I'm feeling rather nervous, though. Today our tour bus will take us up into the mountains, which are cold and snowy, even though it's June. They've offered us a chance to go skiing, which I haven't done since I

*was a child—and the Missouri Ozarks aren't nearly
as big as the mountains of Norway! Still, when I'm
traveling, I've decided to live by the words of an old
and dear friend who once told me, "Test yourself—
you'll never regret it."*

I closed the journal and looked out at the
sparkling water.

I stood up. If I was going to do this, I knew I'd
better hurry before I lost my nerve. I ran down the
beach as fast as I could, into the water, past Dad and
toward Mom and Zac . . . and then BOOM! I got hit by
a wall of water.

It wasn't really that big, but it was strong
enough to knock me over. I went down and rolled
under the wave, bumping against the ocean's sandy
floor. I swallowed salt water and scraped my knee.
It felt like I was under for minutes, when it was
probably only seconds—but when I finally came
up for air, I had water in my nose and it hurt, like
it was going into my brain.

At last I managed to stand, but my legs felt like
jelly. I was gasping and shaking. There was sand in

my eyes, and it stung. I could make out someone
racing toward me.

"Are you all right, Lea?" Dad asked. He wrapped
his arms around me and held me tight so that the
waves couldn't knock us down.

"I'm okay," I sputtered as I leaned into him.
"I think I'll just go sit for a while."

I headed back through the soft sand to the
safety of our beach chairs. I wrapped my beach
towel tightly around myself and turned my back
to the water. I was never going near the ocean again.

Dinner in Distress
Chapter 6

D inner was a welcome distraction to get my mind off being tossed in the ocean like socks in a washing machine. But the menu was written entirely in Portuguese, and I couldn't figure out what was in any of the dishes.

"How do you say 'hamburger' in Portuguese?" I asked my brother.

Mom shook her head. "We didn't come all this way so you could order something you can get at home," she reminded me.

"Brazilian food is great," Zac insisted. "You should try the *moqueca*."

I wrinkled my nose. "The mo—what?"

"Moqueca," Zac repeated. "It's a seafood stew."

Dad made a big show of putting down his menu. "Why don't you order for all of us?" he said, slapping

Zac on the back with pride.

"You got it!" Zac said, smiling. He turned to our waitress and placed our order in rapid Portuguese.

"*Obrigado*," Zac exclaimed. The waitress smiled broadly in response.

"What does 'obrigado' mean?" I asked Zac.

"Thank you," he said as he unfolded his napkin and placed it in his lap.

"For what?" I said. Didn't he listen to anything I said anymore?

Zac laughed. "Cricket, obrigado means 'thank you' in Portuguese—but you would say *obrigada*, because you're a girl."

Oh. "I knew that's what you meant," I fibbed. "I was just kidding."

When a huge iron skillet was set in the middle of our table, I was dubious. What were those suspicious-looking lumps—and what exactly had caused the creamy stew to turn orange? Was it *supposed* to be that color? Well, at least the rice looked familiar.

"It looks delicious!" Mom reached for a serving spoon. "I'm starving. Swimming always makes me hungry. What about you, Lea?"

I made a face. The dish looked weird, and I wasn't sure I wanted to try it. But Zac was watching me, so I piled rice on my plate and then dug into the skillet. I could make out plump shrimp and chunks of tomato in the thick broth. Maybe this would be good after all. I mean, Ama had eaten pickled fish for breakfast in Norway and liked it, and when she was in Korea, she ate beef tripe stew, and loved it! I doubted that I would have felt the same way, but since I like shrimp, I decided this was worth a try.

"Mmm!" Mom said, savoring a bite. "There's crab in there, too."

Over his plate, Zac sprinkled pinches of spices from the trio of small ceramic bowls on the table, ending with a spoonful of clear green sauce swimming with chopped onions.

I reached for the green sauce.

"You might want to go easy there," Zac warned.

I poured the onions and spices over my meal. "I'm just doing what you're doing," I pointed out.

"Yes, but I've been here for months so I'm used to spicy food. It might be too much for you, Cricket."

Urgg. What was his problem? Did he really

think I couldn't handle a few spices? Looking straight at him, I slowly put a huge forkful of moqueca into my mouth.

As I began to chew, it was slightly spicy, but nothing I couldn't handle. I smiled at Zac, who was watching me. But before I knew it, there was a fire in my mouth that made my eyes water. Soon I was sweating, my nose was running, and I thought my head was going to explode.

"Water! Water," I cried out as I fanned my mouth.

Mom handed me my glass of water, then hers, then Dad's and Zac's.

"Água de coco, por favor!" Zac shouted to the waitress. Moments later she appeared with coconut water. "Drink this," he ordered. "It will work better than regular water."

There was no time to argue as I gulped down the cold drink. As my mouth began to cool, I was able to breathe.

"Maybe now you'll listen to your big brother," Zac said as he signaled to the waitress to bring me a clean plate.

In that moment, I hated him.

I took another sip of coconut water to cool my palate—and my temper. As Dad discreetly scraped some of the spices off his food, I saw a girl about my age with glossy, dark hair sitting with her mother. She was watching our table, probably because of the scene I had just made. But instead of turning her nose up at me, she smiled warmly and waved. I gave her a shy wave back.

My attention returned to our table mid-conversation when I heard Mom say my name. "Is that all right with you, Zac?" she continued.

"Are you serious?" Zac looked shocked, like he had been asked to grow a horn on his head or something. "I thought my babysitting days were over."

I must have missed something. "What are you talking about?" I asked, looking back and forth from Mom to Zac.

"They want me to spend the morning looking after you tomorrow while *they* go sea kayaking," Zac said. "Can you believe it?"

"Thanks," I mumbled. "You really know how to make me feel good." I turned to Mom. "Why can't we come kayaking with you?"

"You have to be over twelve to go sea kayaking," Mom said gently. "And I thought the two of you would like to spend time together, too. It's just for a few hours."

"What are your rates these days?" Dad asked Zac. "I'm sure they've gone up from when you were in high school."

Wait! What? "Your rates?" I asked Zac. "You were *paid* to hang out with me?"

"Not always," my brother said nonchalantly. "But sometimes."

"And all this time I thought you had *wanted* to spend time with me," I said. I could feel my cheeks turn red, and it wasn't from the spicy food. "Now I find out that Mom and Dad had to *pay* you to be around me?"

"Chill, Lea," Zac said. "Mom and Dad paid for things like my cell phone, and in exchange I'd babysit you, run errands for them, stuff like that. It's no big deal."

But it *was* a big deal to *me.* I felt as if my whole relationship with my brother had been turned upside down.

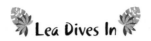

"Don't take it personally," he whispered, messing up my hair. "Cricket, I always had a great time with you. You were such a silly little kid, always making me laugh."

How could I not take it personally? Was I *still* just a "silly little kid" to him? And now my brother was being forced to be my babysitter once again. I wasn't sure who was more annoyed, him or me.

I was still fuming when Dad changed the subject. He pulled out his guidebook and spread a stack of brochures on the table.

"What's on the agenda for tomorrow afternoon?" he asked as he sorted through them.

"Part of me wants to try surfing," Mom said, sounding unsure. "And the other part says I'm too old for things like that."

"Ama was jumping out of airplanes when she was seventy-five," Zac reminded her. "She wasn't too old for anything. Isn't that right, Cricket?"

I shrugged. He was right about Ama, but I didn't feel like agreeing with him about *anything* right then.

"I want to learn how to sleep on the beach," Dad joked.

Zac nudged me. "What about the turtle sanctu-
ary? You'd like that, wouldn't you?" I could tell he
was trying to get on my good side.

When Zac lived at home, one of our favorite
things to do together was to go to the St. Louis Zoo.
As we looked at all the animals, we'd try to act like
them. I loved it when we'd clasp our hands together
and let our arms swing, like an elephant's trunk. Zac
especially liked pretending to be chimpanzees picking the bugs out of each other's hair. I always wanted
to bring an animal home with me, but Zac would
remind me that we couldn't have pets because Dad is
allergic to fur.

"But what about an alligator?" I once asked.
"They don't have fur. And it could live in the bathtub."

"They are pretty cool," he'd agreed. "But if we
had an alligator in the bathtub, how would we ever
take a bath? And what if it climbed out of the tub and
went for you when you were brushing your teeth?"

"Or using the toilet!" I put in, giggling
hysterically.

For my birthday that year, I was thrilled
when Zac gave me a turtle. Ginger lived in my

room in a terrarium that I placed near the window. That way, she had a nice view of Lafayette Square, the old maple trees lining the block, and all the colorful houses.

Thinking about that day warmed up my chilly mood. It occurred to me that Zac had given Ginger to me because he knew I could handle taking care of her. And I realized that even if my parents had paid Zac to hang out with me, they didn't have to pay him to love me. I finally gave my brother a half smile, and in return he gave me a wink.

"Turtles, turtles, turtles," Dad said. He began riffling through his thick pile of brochures. "Helicopter tours . . . parasailing . . . *turtle sanctuary*!" He triumphantly held up a pamphlet with a giant sea turtle on the front.

That night, back at the hotel, I logged on to my e-mail and was surprised by how many messages were waiting for me. Ben, who sat behind me at school, asked if I had wrestled any alligators. Abby gave me a full report on how Ginger was

doing and added, "She doesn't seem at all home-sick." Ms. Swain wanted to know how I was enjoying Brazil and if I had decided what my extra-credit assignment would be.

How could I possibly pick one topic? There was the historic old section of Salvador, the beautiful beaches, the turtle sanctuary tomorrow, and, of course, we'd be heading to the rainforest next week!

I touched my compass necklace to make sure it was still around my neck, and thought of Ama's travel journal. I was up to a part where she was describing a trip to India. She had pasted in a photo of herself sitting on the back of an elephant. She looked so small compared to the elephant, but her smile was huge. Reading about my grandmother's adventures made me feel almost as if I were there with her.

That's when it hit me. For my Brazil assignment I'd create a travel journal, like Ama's. Only, instead of old-fashioned writing in a notebook, I'd do a classroom blog and include photos of my trip!

I hit reply and began to type:

 # Lea Dives In

Dear Ms. Swain,

*I'm having a great time in Brazil and would like to
share my experiences with the class. What if I created
a blog for my extra-credit project and called it "Olá,
Brasil!" I'll write about what I've seen and done, and
I'll include lots of photos . . .*

A Babysitter in Brazil
Chapter 7

The next morning after breakfast, we left the hotel and headed into town, walking past rows of shops that leaned tightly against one another as if they were all one big happy family.

I was still slightly irked about the fact that Mom and Dad thought I still needed a babysitter. Couldn't they have called Zac something else, like my personal assistant? Or my bodyguard?

When my parents headed off to rent sea kayaks, I asked Zac if we could go shopping.

"Shopping? We're at the beach in Brazil—not at the mall. We should go parasailing. Or snorkeling! Or—"

"But look at all these cute little shops! I want to get something with my birthday money."

"Seriously? You come all this way to see the

wonders of Brazil, and now you just want to shop?"

Zac was wrong about my coming all this way
to see the wonders of Brazil. Sure, I had been looking
forward to it—but the real reason I had wanted to
visit Brazil so badly was to spend time with *him*.
I had thought he'd feel the same way, but apparently
I was wrong about that.

"Don't forget you're getting *paid* to hang out
with me," I teased. "That makes *me* the boss."

Zac rolled his eyes and sighed, but I decided not
to let his bad attitude ruin my day.

All around us, the shops bustled with tourists.
They were speaking all sorts of languages I couldn't
understand, but the laughter sounded just like it did
in St. Louis. Laughter—a universal language. Hey,
my first travel discovery! Maybe I could put that in
my blog.

In the center of town was a statue of a beautiful mermaid wearing piles of necklaces, her dark
hair flowing. I stopped to gaze at her. She seemed so
serene, and yet confident.

"You coming?" Zac called out impatiently.

I took a photo of the mermaid, and for a moment

I imagined what she'd look like if she came to life and was swimming in the sea.

"Cricket!" Zac snapped me out of my daydream, and I ran to catch up to him.

Some of the cramped and cozy shops had so much merchandise that it spilled out onto tables outside. One of the friendly shopkeepers beckoned me to a display of handmade jewelry and spoke to me in Portuguese. I turned to Zac to interpret, but he was still standing at the previous shop, looking at T-shirts on display outside.

"Zac?" I called out.

"Just a minute!" he called back as he held up a green shirt with a soccer ball on it.

Great! He kept telling *me* to hurry, and now here *he* was lagging behind when I needed him.

The shopkeeper repeated what she had said more slowly, but I just shrugged and smiled awkwardly, and then took out my camera and started taking pictures. After the first couple of photos, including one of the shopkeeper smiling at me, I began to loosen up and enjoy myself. No matter where I am, I always feel at home when I'm taking photos.

I took lots of pictures of the colorful stores, crammed from floor to ceiling with trinkets and treasures. Some sold glossy postcards of the ocean and palm trees, seashells with "Brasil" painted on them, and wooden turtle key chains. Others had paintings and sculptures by local artists. In one shop a woman was weaving purses to sell, and in another, beautiful handmade necklaces and bracelets fashioned from local plants and nuts sat next to exquisite pearl earrings. Yet another store was stocked with citrus- and melon-scented soaps that smelled so good I was tempted to take a bite out of them.

We paused at a clothing store with *"Moda Praia"* painted in fancy lettering on the sign. Colorful wish ribbons adorned the doorway, and vibrant patterns on the simple clothes made them look like pieces of artwork. I just had to go in.

Zac groaned. "How long is this going to take?" he asked, wearing his I-am-totally-bored face.

I ignored him and pushed open the shop's door.

The lady at the counter smiled. "Olá!" she said brightly. She looked familiar, but I couldn't quite place her.

"Olá," I replied with a smile.

Across the store I spotted a dress so beautiful that it made my heart skip a beat. Layers of magenta, yellow, purple, and green looked like a festival of color. I had always admired the clothes Ama brought home from her many journeys. Whenever she showed up at a school event, I could bet that my grandmother would be the only person wearing a caftan from West Africa or a kimono from Japan. Abby would be so excited if she saw me wearing this dress! She always says I should wear more color.

"What do you think of this one?" I asked Zac, holding the dress up in front of me.

"It's perfect," he said, not even bothering to look.

I rolled my eyes and hung the dress back up. I could always come back later, maybe with Mom.

"Thank you—obrigada," I said to the shopkeeper, trying out the word that Zac had taught me at the restaurant last night.

"Finally!" my brother exclaimed as we walked into the blinding sunshine. It took my eyes a few moments to adjust. "Are you done shopping yet?" he asked, not even hiding the boredom in his voice.

Lea Dives In

I nodded and saw Zac's mood shift from dour to ecstatic.

"Awesome!" he exclaimed. "Let's go back to the hotel so you can change. I'm already wearing my swim trunks."

I had to think fast—the last thing I wanted was to make a fool of myself again in the ocean in front of Zac. "Um, that's okay," I said. "Let's just go straight to the beach."

Zac scratched the back of his head. "Are you sure? I don't mind going back to the hotel."

Now that he was being nice to me, I felt a wave of guilt wash over me for dragging him to all the stores. "You've been waiting for me all morning. I don't want to stand between you and the ocean any longer."

He broke into a wide smile. "Thanks, Cricket."

I smiled back at him, even though his enthusiasm left no doubt that he was more excited to get to the beach than to hang out with me.

Camila

Chapter 8

When we got to the beach, the sand was soft and Zac was instantly barefoot. About a half second later, so was I. As we walked, the sand beneath me grew firmer and harder. I glanced down. Flat expanses of pocked brown rock jutted toward the sea for what seemed like blocks and blocks. It looked like the surface of the moon.

"How does it feel to walk on the bottom of the ocean?" Zac asked.

I shook my head in confusion. Was he teasing me again?

"It's low tide right now," he explained. "In a few hours, when the tide comes in, this will all be covered with water."

Zac knelt down and motioned for me to join him. "Look," he said, pointing into a shallow pool.

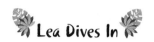

A shell stirred and scampered away.

"What was that?" I asked, reaching for my camera.

Zac lit up. "Look closer," he said.

I leaned in. Other shells were moving, too. And they seemed to have legs. They weren't just shells, but hermit crabs!

Zac waved me over to another small pool of water. It was less than a foot around and only a few inches deep—and filled with a parade of pastel colors.

"That's coral," Zac explained. "I learned about this in my oceanography class. It looks like rock, but it's actually living and provides shelter for a lot of fish and other creatures."

"Look!" I exclaimed, pointing. A tiny black fish darted around quickly, before retreating behind some nubby pink coral.

Instinctively, I started snapping pictures. But when I looked at the photos, I realized I was only photographing my own reflection on the surface of the water. That's when I remembered that my camera was waterproof!

The camera had been a gift from Ama for my

tenth birthday. When I first opened the box, I was excited, but also confused—where could I possibly use an underwater camera in St. Louis?

"Is this to use at the pool?" I asked.

"The pool, the bathtub, streams, rivers, lakes, oceans," Ama said, sneaking a taste of lemon buttercream frosting off my birthday cake. "You never know when you'll need a camera that can shoot on land and sea. You're an award-winning photographer, Lea—you should have a good camera!"

"But Ama, how am I supposed to use an underwater camera without going underwater?" She knew that I preferred to swim freestyle with my face above the surface.

"I didn't even learn how to swim until I was twice your age," she replied. "You're capable of more than you know, Lea."

She saw the doubt in my eyes and gave me a hug. "We'll work on it together," Ama promised. "You'll use that camera underwater someday when the time is right. There's no hurry."

But Ama passed away before she had a chance to fulfill her promise.

I dipped my camera lens into the water. Inches beneath the glassy surface of the tide pool I witnessed another world. My camera captured scenes I could not even see from the surface. Plants sprouted out of the bumpy, multicolored coral, where small fish and other creatures sought refuge.

As I made my way across the tide pools with my camera, I marveled at this new world revealing itself to me. It reminded me of the dioramas we had made in third grade, each a scene from a story we had read. Inside each tide pool were hundreds of stories. I could have spent hours exploring. Maybe I did. I lost track of time.

I stood up and looked around for Zac. He was on the shore sitting on some rocks, and his hair was wet.

"Did you go in the water?" I asked as I made my way toward him.

"Just a quick swim," he said. "Mostly I've been sitting here and watching the waves. Did you get your pictures?"

I nodded and sat down next to him. "Lots of them," I said. "Want to see?" I was anxious to

show off my photography skills.

"Maybe later," he said. "I'm starved. Are you hungry?"

I pretended to look out at the ocean to disguise how hurt I felt that he wasn't interested in my photos. *Just when I thought things between us were getting back to normal . . .*

"Yeah, sure," I said sullenly, making no attempt to hide my disappointment.

"Great—I'll go get lunch. You can wait here if you want." He stood up and stretched before running down the beach toward a food stand.

I sighed and decided to take more photos while I waited for him. There were lots of families around—some were sprawled on beach towels, others sat under the shade of umbrellas staked into the sand—and they were every kind of color and complexion I could imagine. It was as if people from every part of the world had all gathered on the beach in Brazil. I started taking photos for my blog. I took some photos of one family that all had the same red hair, same red sunburn, and same British accent. There were a lot of people in the

water, including children much younger than me.

I trained my camera on a swimmer making
her way toward the shore with long, strong strokes.
What I would have given to be able to swim like that!
As she pulled herself out of the water, I realized that
she was the same girl who had been at the restaurant
the night before. The one who had waved to me. She
caught me staring at her, and a flash of recognition
shone on her face.

"Olá!" she shouted. She broke into a jog, heading
straight for me.

"Olá?" I said tentatively. Did she remember what
a fool I had made of myself with the super-spicy
stew?

The girl's brown eyes were shining. She wrung
out her wet hair and fashioned it in a tight bun without even using clips or a rubber band.

"*Olá, meu nome é Camila! Você está visitando?*" she
said in a rush.

I opened my mouth to respond, but nothing
came out. "Um . . . I don't speak Portuguese," I said
apologetically.

The girl let go of a bright giggle. Her smile was

kind, and I could tell that she wasn't laughing *at* me. "I can speak English," she said with a lilting Brazilian accent. "You are from the United States, correct? I think we should be friends, don't you?"

Before I could answer, she exclaimed, "Yes! Let's be friends!"

And that's how I met the whirlwind named Camila Cavalcante.

By the time I spotted Zac heading back with lunch, Camila had already told me all about herself. She had been talking so fast that it was hard to follow her, but from what I could understand, she was ten years old like me, and her mother owned a clothing boutique.

Camila had lots of relatives in Chicago and she visited them every year, which explained why her English was so good. School was out, and she was on her summer vacation.

"I like to swim while my *mãe*, my mother, eats lunch," she explained, waving to someone sitting on a nearby bench. When the woman waved back,

I recognized her from Moda Praia, the clothing store where I had seen the beautiful dress.

Camila was so animated when she spoke. Her hands were in constant motion and she thought nothing of leaning close to talk as if we were sharing secrets. Back home, it usually takes me a long time to make friends since, unlike Zac, I can be kind of quiet around new people. But with Camila, quiet wasn't an option. She asked me a thousand questions, and soon I found myself laughing along with her as if we had been friends for life.

"Olá!" Camila greeted Zac as he came toward us.

"Olá!" he called back. He had his hands full with fresh fruit, savory snacks wrapped in brown paper, and smoothies.

"This is my new friend, Camila—" I started to say. But before I could finish introducing them, Zac and Camila were chattering away in Portuguese. Every time I tried to get a word in, one of them would speak louder or start laughing at something the other said. I couldn't understand either of them. It was as though Zac and Camila were the friends, and I was just some stranger standing awkwardly nearby.

 **Camila**

When they laughed, I tried to laugh along, too. But it was frustrating not to understand what they were saying.

Suddenly Zac's stomach growled so loudly that Camila and I burst out laughing. He blushed and excused himself as he took a big bite of pastry. Now that his mouth was full, I was finally able to continue my conversation with Camila.

She pointed to my wrist. "You have a wish bracelet," she noted. "Orange is for courage."

I tugged at the ribbon, hoping to accidentally-on-purpose loosen one of the three knots. "I'm really hoping it starts working soon," I told her. I thought about my failed attempts at venturing into the ocean. So far, the bracelet had given me nothing but false hope.

I swallowed back the tightness in my throat and bit into a banana. It was smaller than the ones at home and much sweeter.

"You have to have patience," Camila explained. "Sometimes your wish comes true before you even notice it."

I nodded, grateful for Camila's encouragement.

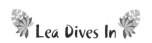

Zac offered Camila some fruit, but she was content just to keep talking. I bit into the other pastry Zac had brought. He told me it was called *pastel de forno*. The tender golden piecrust was folded and crimped so that I could eat it with one hand, and it was stuffed with a deliciously spiced meat that left me wanting more.

Zac polished off the last of his lunch and washed it down with an *açaí* berry smoothie. "Ladies," he said, "if you don't mind, I'll go for a swim while you chat."

Before we could reply, he went off sprinting toward the water.

"You're a really great swimmer," I told Camila as we watched Zac doing the backstroke. "I wish I could swim like you."

She shrugged. "I grew up at the beach. My mother jokes that I could swim before I could walk."

Camila was surprised when I told her that I had never seen the ocean before, and even more surprised when I revealed that I was afraid to put my face in the water. "I got hit by a wave and I thought I was going to drown," I confessed.

 Camila

It was so easy to talk to her.

Instead of laughing, Camila confided, "I am afraid of . . . ," she paused, then whispered, "I'm afraid of heights."

"Lots of people are," I assured her.

I thought about Ama hang gliding in Australia. In her journal she had written that she was nervous at first, so she signed up to hang glide in tandem—with someone else. After a successful, and fun, flight, her nerves melted away, and she couldn't wait to go solo.

"Camila," I asked, "is there someplace near here where the waves aren't quite as big? I really do want to swim in the ocean, but, well—"

Just then, Zac ran up to us and grabbed a towel to dry off. "We're late!"

"Late for what?" I asked.

"Turtles. Remember the turtle sanctuary?"

I had forgotten. Still, as excited as I was to go to the sanctuary, I was sad to leave my new friend. I turned to Camila. "Can we meet again later?"

"*Claro que sim*—of course! I'll be at Moda Praia all afternoon," she said. "Come by when you're free."

I was startled when Camila gave me a huge good-bye hug, but then I hugged her back and we both grinned.

As Zac and I headed back to the hotel, I asked him, "How do you say 'friend' in Portuguese?"

"*Amiga,*" he said.

"*Amiga,*" I repeated. I had made an amiga in Brazil!

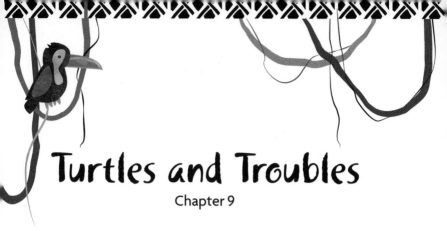

Turtles and Troubles

Chapter 9

Mom and Dad were waiting for us at the hotel. Both looked slightly sunburned and majorly happy.

"We had a great time kayaking!" Dad enthused.

"He wanted to bring a kayak home, but couldn't figure out how to fit it in a suitcase," Mom said, laughing.

"Who's ready to *see* turtles?" my father asked. "Get it? *Sea* turtles . . . "

Zac and I looked at each other and rolled our eyes.

The sanctuary was about a mile away, and we decided to walk. Zac and Dad led the way as Mom and I followed and I told her all about Camila.

We made our way down a closed-off street, and in the distance I could see the entrance for the

turtle sanctuary with a big sign overhead that read *"Amigos do Oceano Santuário das Tartarugas Marinhas."* Dad paid and we got our hands stamped with a cute turtle design.

As the tour guide led us into the sanctuary, I took in all the sights, snapping pictures whenever I could. First we walked through an acrylic walkway cut through the center of a giant aquarium. All around us were turtles, fish, and other sea creatures. It was so cool. *Is this what it's like to swim underwater in the ocean?* I wondered. *Is this what I have been missing?*

We continued down the path, where life-size wooden cutouts of sea turtles towered over me. We passed pristine pools that held the biggest turtles I had ever seen. On the other side of the path, tiny baby turtles waddled around smaller pools. I couldn't wait to write about this in my blog!

The guide stopped and spoke in Portuguese as I took photos for my blog. Zac translated: "Until about thirty years ago, little was known about the sea turtles. They used to be hunted for their meat and eggs and their beautiful shells. We didn't realize that it takes thirty years for them to be old enough to reproduce and that they were becoming endangered. Now there are laws against poaching them and organizations, like *Amigos do Oceano,* that help them."

I looked at the turtles of different colors and sizes, and couldn't help thinking of Ginger. My heart ached at the thought of them ever becoming extinct.

"What about these?" I asked, pointing to the small pool that held the baby turtles. "Is this where they're born?"

Zac turned to the guide and began speaking in Portuguese. As they talked, Zac's voice rose and he looked like he had just won a prize.

"What?" I asked, tapping his shoulder. "Zac, what is he saying?"

At last, my brother and the guide parted. "Guess what!" Zac began excitedly. "Tonight is one of the nights the baby turtles hatch and make their way to the ocean."

My eyes grew big. "Tonight?"

Zac nodded. "The volunteer says we can watch as long as we're respectful of the turtles and don't get in their way."

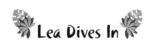

"We can go, right?" I asked Dad. "Please, please, please, please?"

"Hmm," he said, wrinkling his brow. "I'm getting a vague feeling that you want to see the hatchlings?"

"Can we?" I held my breath.

He pointed to Mom. "Ask the boss," he said.

Mom gathered me in her arms. "We wouldn't miss it for the world," she assured me.

Back at the hotel, Zac was antsy. He tapped his fingers on the desk and sighed a lot. He had always hated being cooped up indoors. I ignored him as I wrote my first blog post about the turtle sanctuary. Finally Zac nudged Dad, who had just spread out on the couch. "What are we going to do between now and the turtle hatch tonight?"

"All that kayaking this morning has worn me out," Dad said, yawning. "I think I'll take a nap."

Mom nodded. "I'm going to relax and read."

"Didn't you say you wanted to try surfing?" Zac asked hopefully. "There's still time for the

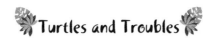
beach before the sun sets."

Mom looked like she was deep in thought.
"Maybe later," she mused. "I'll just read for now."

"I'm almost done with my post, and I told
Camila I'd drop by her mom's store this afternoon,"
I said. "Will you take me, Zac?"

"There's an idea," Mom said, winking at me.
"Zac, go with your sister, all right?"

"Do I even have a choice?" my brother asked.

"No," Mom and Dad said at the same time.

"You owe me, Cricket," Zac sighed as he grabbed
his sunglasses.

Just as she had said she would be, Camila was
helping her mother at Moda Praia. I grinned when
I saw what she was wearing.

"I love your dress," I said. It was the one that
I had admired earlier.

Camila smiled and spun around to show it off.
"Me too!" she said. "It just came in this week."

I knew what I would be spending my birthday
money on.

After introductions, *Senhora* Cavalcante said that Camila could spend the rest of the afternoon with us.

"Let's go!" Camila said to Zac and me. "There's something I want to show you."

She led us through the streets of Praia Tropical, and soon we came upon a cheering crowd that had gathered in the town square. Two men were circling each other, kicking and spinning.

"It's a fight," I gasped, alarmed.

"Actually, it's *capoeira*," Camila explained. "Hear the music? It's a tradition that African slaves brought to Brazil. It's really martial arts, but it looks like a dance, and it's very popular here."

We watched the young men move to the beat of the music and cheered along with the rest of the spectators. It was like kickboxing and ballet, and the two men sparred to the music like athletes on a dance floor. I took out my camera and shot a video to put up on my blog later.

The young men finished with a bow, and the crowd cheered and started to disperse. I had just turned to Camila to ask where she was taking us next when Zac suddenly advanced in my direction

and pretended to take a swing at me.

I backed away and yelled, "What are you doing?!"

"Capoeira?" Zac said, like it was something I should have known.

I felt myself turn red.

Okay, I thought, *I can play this game, too.* So I advanced toward him, then backed away, and he did the same as we circled each other, pretending to land punches and kicks. To be funny, Zac kept tapping me on the top of my head and laughing. Camila laughed, too. But not me. The more he did it the madder I got, until I shoved him hard.

"Hey!" Zac yelled. "What are you doing? I thought we were just playing around!"

"Sorry," I grumbled. But I wasn't.

Camila was bouncing up and down, practicing capoeira with an invisible partner. When Zac turned from me and started sparring with her, she didn't hesitate to duck and take fake swings at him. She was like a whirlwind! Unlike some of the girls in my class who try hard to act cool and not get too excited about things, Camila sparkled with enthusiasm. I wished I could be more like her.

And yet, here I was, upset with Zac for trying to have fun with me. I tried to tell myself to lighten up. But Zac had embarrassed me, and I couldn't shake off my hurt feelings.

"Where are we going now?" Zac asked Camila. They had stopped with the capoeira and were walking together, while I followed along, alone.

"You'll see," Camila said, sounding mysterious.

We were making our way down the beach, and there were fewer and fewer people. Along the shore, hotels and boardwalks had been replaced by coconut trees, wild brush, and steep hills.

Camila broke into a jog. Zac picked up his pace as well, turning to call over his shoulder, "Don't fall too far behind, Cricket!"

"Cricket?" Camila asked me as I caught up with them.

"It's just a dumb nickname," I said, giving Zac a sideways glance. *Seriously, did he have to call me that baby name in front of my new friend?*

"I like it!" Camila said. "Come on, Cricket!"

I bristled. Great, now *she* was calling me Cricket, too.

Turtles and Troubles

As we jogged around a bend, I could make out a little house nestled against the high rocks beside the cliffs. It was a small wooden beach house with a thatched roof. A green hammock hung outside, and swim fins and other water equipment were stacked neatly on shelves by the side of the building. Snorkel masks hung evenly spaced on a clothesline.

"Isn't it wonderful?" Camila asked. "I love it here. The little house is so cozy, and look at this beach!"

It was beautiful. White sand lined the crystal blue ocean, and lush green plants grew against the nearby cliffs. Still, I wasn't sure why we were here. Camila knew how I felt about swimming in the ocean. Had she forgotten? I felt my jaw tense as I tried to smile.

"It's pretty awesome," Zac was saying. "I could totally live here. In fact, when my semester is finished, I think I may just move in and ... and ... "

Zac's sentence trailed off. I followed his gaze to see a young woman about his age coming out of the shack. She had bronze skin, and her wavy black hair was pulled back into a ponytail. So that's what had him all tongue-tied.

"*Oi*, Paloma!" Camila called out. "*Estes são meus amigos.*"

"Olá," I said.

"Oh ... uh ... " Zac stammered, blushing. It was as if my brother had forgotten how to speak. No Portuguese, no English. Nothing.

Camila and I looked at each other and giggled.

"I am Paloma," the young woman said in halting English. "Camila's family."

"She means my cousin," Camila explained. "Paloma, this is Cricket!"

I looked at Camila and said, "Please, call me Lea," before smiling at Paloma.

Camila nodded. "Lea," she said.

"I'm Zac," my brother finally managed to say. "Lea's cousin—er, sister." Much to my delight, the more Paloma smiled, the worse Zac got. "I mean, Lea is my sister," he stammered. "I am her brother. We're brothers."

When we finally stopped giggling, Camila explained why she had brought us here. Her cousin, she said, was a snorkeling instructor and guide, and knew the best places to swim. "Places with calm

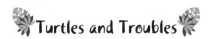

waters," Camila added pointedly.

I gave her a weak smile. I was grateful that Camila had gone to all this trouble to find a place for me to practice swimming underwater. But now, looking out at the expanse of blue water, I was worried I might chicken out.

Then I realized that I had a good excuse not to go in the water. "I'm not wearing a bathing suit under my dress," I said, trying to look disappointed. "So I guess I won't be able to go snorkeling today."

"Oh," Camila said. She said something to Paloma in Portuguese. I looked to Zac to see what she had said, but he remained tongue-tied.

"*Amanhã*," Paloma said.

"Tomorrow," Camila translated. "We'll take you snorkeling tomorrow."

"*Amanhã*," I said, nodding and hoping that my smile looked sincere. But would I be ready tomorrow?

I checked my wish bracelet and was disappointed to find it still firmly attached to my wrist.

I turned to Zac, who was staring at Paloma but would glance away whenever she looked in his direction. "Paloma's going to take me snorkeling

tomorrow, Zac," I said, speaking loudly and slowly. "You don't have to come if you don't want to."

All of a sudden, Zac came alive. In a voice that was slightly too loud, he said, "Of course I'll be there! I, uh, need to accompany Lea and Camila—for their safety, of course."

When we left, Zac shook Paloma's hand and then bowed.

Camila and I tried not to laugh as Paloma looked thoroughly confused and bowed back to Zac.

"Seriously, Zac," I said as we headed back to Moda Praia. "You don't have to come with us tomorrow. I know how much you *hate* having to babysit me."

I was only half joking. The last thing I wanted was to freak out about going underwater in front of my brother and have him think I was a big baby.

"Paloma doesn't have a boyfriend," Camila said, even though he hadn't asked.

Zac perked up. "Dearest sister, I love shopping for dresses with you and watching you stare at tide pools for hours. So wherever you're going tomorrow, you can count on me being right there with you!"

# Turtles and Troubles

I couldn't help laughing, even though I was nervous about having him witness another failed attempt to swim in the ocean.

After we had walked Camila back to Moda Praia and said good-bye, Zac turned to me. "So, Cricket, do you think Paloma liked me?"

I shrugged. "How should I know?" I had to admit it was sort of nice when he wasn't being a bossy know-it-all. I was pleased that my brother was finally asking my opinion of something—even if it was about his crush.

"Listen," Zac said, "be sure to say good things about me to Camila, okay? That way maybe she'll tell Paloma."

"We'll see," I teased. I loved that my brother was asking *me* for a favor. "Hey, any chance you want to go and look at jewelry with me? I'd love to go back to that shop with the necklaces made from nuts."

"No way—" Zac caught himself and pasted on an exaggerated smile. "I mean, sure!" he said, adding with mock seriousness, "You know I'd love that."

Night Surprises
Chapter 10

My parents were in a giddy mood at dinner, and wanted to hear about where we had been for the past couple of hours. When I told them about our snorkeling plans, both were eager to come along.

"We'll be right there with you," Dad said, giving me a small reassuring nod.

I knew that he understood how shaken up I was after getting hit by the wave. Part of me was happy that my parents would be there—but the other part wished they'd be far away in case I had another meltdown. The fewer witnesses, the better.

"What's this snorkeling instructor like?" Mom asked. "You said he's Camila's cousin?"

"Camila's cousin isn't a he, she's a girl. Isn't that right, Zac?" I asked.

My brother, who had been happily munching

on a skewer of barbecued pork, choked and blushed.

Dad slapped him on the back. "You okay, son?"

"Zac, did you use sunscreen today?" Mom asked, leaning in to get a better look at his face.

"He must've stayed in the sun too long," I teased. "But I'll make sure he doesn't get burned tomorrow."

"Why, thank you, Lea," Zac said, his voice dripping with good-natured sarcasm. "You are such a swell sister."

"You are welcome, Zachary," I replied, patting his hand. "And you are the best brother ever."

"I love it that the two of you are getting along so well," Mom said, reaching out, grabbing both our hands, and giving them a squeeze.

Zac and I gave each other big fake smiles. Then I stuck my tongue out at him and he did the same to me. It was like a table version of capoeira.

After dinner, we headed toward the stretch of beach where the sanctuary guide had told us the turtle hatching would take place. Dad and Zac

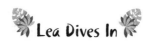

walked several yards ahead while Mom and I hung back to talk.

"It's so nice that you and Zac have made some friends here," Mom said.

"I can't wait for you to meet Camila," I told her. "I feel like I've known her forever."

"And it sounds like Zac is quite taken by this snorkeling instructor you met," she said with a grin.

I shrugged. "I think he's more interested in seeing her than he is in hanging out with his silly little kid sister," I mumbled.

Mom stopped and raised her eyebrows. "Now why would you say that?" she asked, putting her hand on my shoulder.

"Well," I hesitated, "have you noticed anything different about Zac?"

I glanced at him and Dad, who by now were way in front of us. For the first time, I noticed that Zac was taller than my father.

"I suppose he's become more of an adult since he left for Brazil, but he's still the same Zac that we've always loved," Mom said. "Why? Do you think he's changed?"

I nodded. "He's . . . he's . . . I dunno." How could I explain to her how I felt when I couldn't even figure it out myself?

"When we're together, it just doesn't feel the same as back when he lived at home or visited during his college breaks. Things between us are just . . . different." I sighed. "It's almost like he doesn't even want to be around me."

Mom was quiet for a while, and we began walking again, this time in silence. Finally she spoke. "You know, Lea, it's probably true that Zac isn't the same, and that's to be expected—especially when you have a life-altering experience like going to live in Brazil. But have you considered that maybe *you've* changed, too?"

I didn't know how to answer her. What did she mean?

"I'm the same person I've always been," I said defensively. "Besides, I haven't had any life-altering experiences."

"Didn't your life change when Zac went off to college? That was a really hard change for you. You were only seven then. Now you're ten and in fifth

grade. And in those three years, you really have grown up. You're not my little girl anymore," Mom said, her eyes twinkling. "And maybe Zac doesn't see that yet. But he will, if you give him a chance."

Maybe she was right. Maybe I needed to show Zac that I was no longer the little girl he'd left behind in St. Louis. But how?

We continued down the beach, watching the golden sun melt behind the cliffs that ran along the shore. Finally we came upon a small crowd milling around a rectangular patch of sand cordoned off by a band of plastic tape. The sanctuary volunteer came over to greet us, and said that the hatching would begin soon. It took forever for the sun to set and the moon to rise, but at last a veil of darkness blanketed the beach.

The volunteer spoke in a whisper as Zac translated. "Usually, lights from the buildings lining the beach would shine bright at night. But the turtle sanctuary volunteers have worked with the hotels to shield their lights during nesting season. The hatchlings use the moon and the sun to find the sea and would be very disoriented if the building lights

were at their full brightness. The baby turtles would head to the hotels instead of the ocean."

The thought of thousands of hatchlings entering the lobby of our hotel was so funny that I couldn't help giggling.

Zac gave me a stern look. "Stop goofing off, Cricket!"

I was glad it was dark out and no one could see my face burn red. *Did he have to say that? And so loudly?*

"I'm not goofing off!" I hissed. "And stop calling me—"

"Shhh," the volunteer warned, pointing to the sand a few feet ahead of us. "Look!"

I tamped down my temper as the sand began to shift. At first it was scary, like the ground was coming alive. But soon, hundreds, maybe thousands of little turtle heads popped up. My frustration with Zac was replaced by a wave of excitement as the baby turtles emerged from the sand.

"The eggs are hidden under the sand," Zac whispered, as the volunteer explained. "The hatch-lings break free from their leathery shells, and the

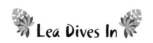

shells harden. Then the turtles create a space under the shells and wait for their brothers and sisters to hatch. When all the eggs have hatched, the hatchlings start digging. Somehow they know when it's nighttime—experts think they can sense the temperature dropping—and that's when they come out from the sand."

More and more baby turtles emerged onto the beach and began waddling toward the sea. It was like a parade. Hope was in the air. The babies were small, no bigger than my hand, yet their determination was huge.

"They head to the brightest spot on the horizon," Zac continued. "And that's the moon over the waves. They can actually sense the direction of the sea as they scurry toward it. They have to be fast because they are easy prey for crabs and seagulls and other birds. The babies enter the water and let the waves carry them away as they swim for their lives."

Instinctively, I reached for Ama's compass. It was as if the turtles had their own internal compasses that would protect them and lead them home.

The hatchlings all looked a lot like my pet turtle,

Night Surprises

Ginger. I wanted to scoop them all into my arms and carry them to safety, but we had to stand back and let nature take its course, and not interfere. So instead, I raised my camera and began to take some photos for my blog. I knew that my classmates would be in awe of this!

I had turned off my flash because it would confuse the babies, so I used the moon as my light—just like the hatchlings did. I also shot a short video of a hatchling making its way into the welcoming ocean waves. Soon he floated off, never to be seen again. Well, not to be seen again that night, anyway. I hoped that he would grow big and strong and be right at home in the warm Brazilian waters, like the turtle that swam with Ama in Hawaii.

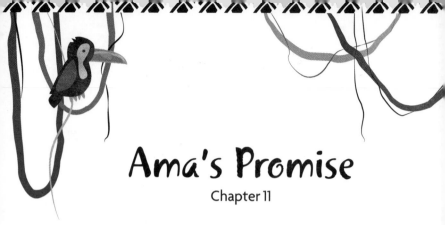

Ama's Promise

Chapter 11

Last night was my third night in Kenya. I woke up in the middle of the night, restless. I unzipped my tent to go out for a stretch. The tents around me were dark as my tour group slept. The moon and stars shone brightly over the savanna and all was quiet. Then I heard something that I'd never heard before: a deep, low rumbling sound. At first, I thought it might be one of my tour mates snoring. But then the sound grew closer. Instinctively, I knew to get back in my tent.

The next morning my safari guide showed the group a path of paw prints in the dirt just a few yards away from our camp. We'd had visitors during the night: a pride of lions!

I closed Ama's journal and turned off the

reading light next to my bed. As I listened to Mom and Dad snore, I wondered if I'd ever get to sleep myself. I shivered, thinking about Ama's close call with the lions.

When I eventually fell asleep, I dreamed that I was wading into the ocean. The water was already up to my waist when I noticed that the waves were growing bigger and stronger. Afraid, I decided to head back to shore, but when I turned around, I saw that there were lions waiting for me on the sand.

I was relieved when I woke up safe and dry in a warm bed! That is, until I remembered that today we were going snorkeling. And I didn't think there was any way that I could snorkel without facing that scary almost-drowning feeling again.

What had I been thinking when I agreed to this? Zac would probably call me a chicken, Camila would know I was a coward, and my parents and Paloma would witness my shame at being afraid to swim in the sea.

"Get up, Cricket," Zac yelled, swatting me over the head with a pillow. "Let's go!"

"Stop it," I grumbled. By then, I was imagining

all the people of Brazil laughing at me.

"Come on," he urged. "We're all ready and just waiting for you."

That morning, if there had been a race between a snail, a sloth, and me, I would have lost.

In the hotel cafe, Dad and Zac wolfed down their breakfast, and Mom kept me company while I nibbled on some crusty bread that I had slathered with guava jelly.

"I've never seen anyone eat breakfast that slowly," my mother noted. She was on her third cup of coffee. "Any slower and we may miss our snorkeling date!" she joked.

She didn't realize that that was my *plan*.

By the time we got back to the room, I was stuffed with *pão francês*, having eaten three of the small loaves of bread.

"Hey!" Dad said. "I read in the guidebook that there's a shipwreck somewhere around here but only the locals know where it is. Think anyone will mistake me for a local?"

Zac and I looked at his sunburned face and his new *I Love Brazil* T-shirt and *Brazil Nut* cap.

We both burst out laughing.

"Lea, get your bathing suit and let's go!" Mom said cheerfully.

"I can't find it," I said as I pretended to look in my suitcase.

Immediately my mother began searching the room. She is always the finder of lost things at home.

"Got it!" she cried triumphantly, waving the bathing suit in the air. "But what I don't understand is what it was doing behind the dresser."

I shrugged. "That's so weird," I said, making a mental note to find a better hiding place for it next time.

Camila and Zac chatted in rapid-fire Portuguese as they led the way to Paloma's beach shack. Mom and Dad lagged behind, flipping through Dad's guidebook to plan the afternoon's activities. I was in the middle, by myself, thinking about Ama's near miss with the lions in the African savanna. I looked at my orange wish bracelet. Would I ever be as brave or adventurous as my grandmother?

# Lea Dives In

As we headed along the beach, I hung back and busied myself taking photos of the ocean and of the surfers and paddleboarders on the horizon.

After a while, Dad let go of Mom's hand and came over to me.

"How are you doing, Lea?" he asked.

"Fine," I said. I looked at my brother, who was now making monkey noises and cracking Camila up.

"It's great to see Zac, isn't it?" he asked.

I nodded.

"Are you excited about snorkeling?"

I nodded again.

"I see," Dad said. "You know, Lea, it's okay to be scared, especially when it's something new. In fact, it keeps us on our toes. We pay more attention when we're scared."

"I'm not scared," I said unconvincingly.

"Well, you don't have to do anything you don't want to do," Dad continued. "But you've been talking about swimming in the ocean since we started planning this trip to Brazil last fall. You didn't come all this way just to sit on a beach chair, did you?" When I didn't say anything, he went on. "I'll be

there when we go snorkeling, and so will Zac and Mom. We're not going to let anything bad happen to you. I mean, think about it," he added, looking serious. "If anything happened to you, then who would laugh at my jokes?"

I couldn't help chuckling. "Thanks, Dad," I said, giving him a hug.

As we neared the beach shack, Zac began to quiet down, and soon he wasn't saying a word. Paloma ran out and greeted us warmly as Camila introduced her to my parents. I was surprised when Paloma hugged me as if we were old friends. Meanwhile Zac pretended to be interested in the snorkeling fins that were piled up on a low wooden bench.

"Zac!" Paloma cried. "Olá!"

He looked up as if surprised to see her. "Olá, Paloma," he replied, turning red.

I nudged him playfully and reminded him, "Don't forget to use sunscreen."

Zac had lost his voice, Paloma's English was spotty, and my parents' and my Portuguese was practically nonexistent, so Camila translated for her cousin. She explained that we would be walking for about half a mile to a quiet cove where the water was calm and smooth as glass. Before we left, we each grabbed our snorkeling equipment: a face mask, flippers, and a snorkel with a rubber mouthpiece.

Paloma led the way, with Zac trailing close behind like a puppy. After a while they were side by side, and he seemed to have recovered his voice. Soon he was making her laugh, and his normal fun-loving nature was on overdrive.

Dad grabbed my hand and gave it a "you-can-do-it" squeeze. I gave him an "I-hope-so" squeeze back.

We were the only ones on the beach. Every time I thought we'd stop, Paloma kept going. Finally, as we walked around a bend, we all let out a collective "Ooooh!"

"We are here!" she announced.

The sand looked like white frosting, and the turquoise sea sparkled under the bright sunlight. Lush coconut palm trees lined the beach. I whipped out my camera to photograph the small monkeys

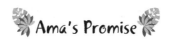

playing on their branches. They were so cute, darting here and there, chasing each other. I could have watched them for hours, but Camila was already handing me a snorkel and mask to put on.

Paloma paired each of us with the right size of snorkeling equipment. I had a hard time slipping the rubber fins on my feet. When I got up and tried to walk around, I felt like an awkward duck. I kept tripping in the sand and almost fell a couple of times. I started to get embarrassed until I saw that no one in my family was very graceful with the fins on!

Together, we all waddled to the water's edge. There, we cleaned off our masks, and then adjusted them to fit around our heads. I had trouble with mine, but Paloma was patient and showed me how to tighten the band so that it would fit snugly.

As we entered the ocean, Dad stayed by my side, but I only waded in up to my knees. Then I froze. Something was stopping me again.

I watched Mom, Zac, and Camila swimming confidently, using their fins, faces down in the water, snorkels up in the air.

"Go ahead," I said to Dad.

"I'm fine right here," he said.

Paloma, who had been snorkeling with the others, came back and joined us. "How does the snorkel feel?" she asked, pointing to it.

I put the snorkel's mouthpiece into place. It felt funny in my mouth and reminded me of when I was at the dentist getting my teeth X-rayed. I had to admit that I was looking forward to snorkeling with the same enthusiasm that I had for going to the dentist.

"You look great," Dad said. "We should take a picture of this."

That reminded me! Quickly, I turned and duck-walked back to my beach towel to get my camera, tripping and falling over myself with those huge fins on my feet.

"You go," Paloma suggested to Dad, as she motioned to Zac and Mom. "Lea can swim with me."

"You're sure?" Dad asked. He looked at me.

I nodded with the snorkel in my mouth and my camera's strap around my wrist.

Slowly, I followed Paloma into the warm water.

Ama's Promise

By the time I was waist-deep, my stomach felt like it was doing somersaults, but I repeated Ama's mantra in my head: *Test yourself. You'll never regret it.*

I thought of the hatchlings—the tiny sea turtles making their way across the sand, facing danger at every step. The sea was their one chance at safety. Here I was, scared that I might get salt water in my nose, and those baby turtles were risking their lives to make it into the Atlantic Ocean.

With Paloma holding my hand, I slowly lowered my head until I put my face in the water. With the mask on I was able to keep my eyes open, and I began breathing through the snorkel. I let go of Paloma, pushed off with the fins, and started kicking. The fins worked much better in the water than on the sand, and suddenly I realized I was swimming in the ocean.

I used my fins to propel me farther. At first, all I saw was the rippled sand below, and the water was so shallow that I could touch the bottom of the ocean with the tip of my fin. But before long, Paloma and I reached the reef. Below us were walls of colorful pastel coral. Lush green plants swayed

slowly back and forth, as if dancing to their own music. Fish, big and small, swam past. Some flashed by in a hurry; others floated lazily along, taking their time. In the distance I could see Zac diving under the water with Camila. My parents swam near the surface, and when Dad gave me a big thumbs-up, I returned it.

In the beginning it was hard to swim and take photos at the same time, but soon I got the hang of it. Up close, the coral reefs looked like multicolored bubbles of rocks—reds and pinks, blues and greens. At first when fish swam toward me, I'd flinch. But after a while I started taking photos of the fish staring at me staring at them. I was so glad I had my underwater camera!

I thought again to my last birthday. When Ama gave me the camera, I couldn't understand why I'd need it, because she knew how I felt about swimming underwater. "We'll work on it together," she had promised, but she had died before we ever got the chance.

Now, as I continued to swim and take photos, that's when it occurred to me: By giving me her

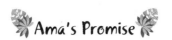

Ama's Promise

journals, Ama was with me in spirit—it was her words that had helped me push past my fear. And she was right: I had tested myself, and I would never regret it. Ama *had* kept her promise.

An Invitation
Chapter 12

Once we returned to shore, I realized that I had never been so hungry in my life. Paloma had brought fresh melon and pineapple slices, and *saltenha*, a flaky pastry filled with spicy meat and raisins. The air seemed to sparkle with excitement as everyone talked at once.

"Did you see the schools of those fish with yellow stripes?"

"The coral was like an explosion of color!"

"Was it an eel or a small snake that was darting out of the plants?"

"I've never seen anything like that before—I can't wait to go snorkeling again," I exclaimed, surprising even myself.

After lunch, Mom and Dad headed back to the hotel for some rest while Zac and I stayed at the beach with Camila and Paloma. Zac was acting so goofy around Paloma that I felt as if the tables had turned and *I* was babysitting *him*!

"I'd love to go snorkeling again," I told Paloma. "Do you think we can go tomorrow?"

"That's a great idea," Zac chimed in. Then he said something in Portuguese and had Paloma and Camila laughing so hard they couldn't breathe.

"What did he say?" I asked Camila.

She leaned in close and said, "He said that if you can't snorkel again, you will shrivel up and turn sour, so she must agree to take you both snorkeling again."

"Oh, right, for *my* sake," I said with a smirk at Zac. But at least we both agreed that going snorkeling again was a *must*.

While Zac and Paloma talked, I showed Camila some of my photos. "These are amazing, Lea!" she said. "I've lived here all my life, but some of these are like I'm seeing Praia Tropical for the first time."

I showed her more of the photos I had taken on

our trip, and stopped at the image of the mermaid statue I had seen while I was shopping with Zac.

"Her name is Yemanjá. She's the Queen of the Sea," Camila explained. "She's an *orixá*, a sea goddess from African traditions. She watches over the fishermen, keeps them safe, and brings good luck. Yemanjá also protects children, sailors, and the sea. There's a festival in her honor on the second of February—that's this Tuesday. You should go with me!" Her eyes were shining bright. "Please say you'll come."

"Tuesday," I said, thinking out loud. "That's the day we leave to visit Zac's host family in a town near the rainforest. But I'll see if I can go for at least part of it."

"You'll love it," Camila said. "People bring flowers, perfume, jewelry, and other trinkets to please Yemanjá. The fishermen gather the gifts in baskets and take them out to sea. Legend says, the gifts that sink have been accepted by Yemanjá. When this happens, it guarantees another year of good blessings for all!"

It sounded amazing. Suddenly I had a twinge of

sadness thinking about how much Ama would have loved being part of this tradition. I remembered the time Ama came home from India without her favorite watch. "Where is it?" I had asked, touching her wrist.

She smiled. "I left it in India," she told me. "I had a tour guide who was absolutely marvelous. But his watch had broken, so I gave him mine. He needed it more than I did."

"But you loved that watch," I protested.

"I still do," she said. "But Lea, when you visit a place, you don't just take—you leave something behind."

Then she told me about the other things she had left in the places she visited, such as her gooey butter cake recipe that she wrote down for a baker in Paris, and a copy of *Around the World in Eighty Days* that she "lent" to a woman on a train in Istanbul, and a pair of sunglasses that she gave to a little boy in the Maldives.

As we all started packing up our snorkeling gear to head back to Paloma's shack, I wondered, *What would Ama offer to Yemanjá?*

The Hike
Chapter 13

As the week went on, I made sure we had some beach time every day. Soon it was hard for me to believe I had ever been scared of going underwater. I was still wary of the waves, but had learned how to swim under the big ones rather than let them knock me over. And I always brought my camera with me—just in case I spotted one of the baby sea turtles swimming through the waves.

My classmates were impressed by the photos I posted on the class blog. I even took some underwater selfies with fish swimming past! When a couple of annoying boys in my class accused me of editing the photos on my computer to make them more impressive, I took that as the ultimate compliment.

One evening as I was uploading more photos to my blog, Mom came and sat next to me. "You're

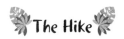

really a skillful photographer, Lea," she said, looking over my shoulder at a photo I had just posted of a teenage boy surfing. The boy was riding the crest of a wave and there was pure joy on his face.

"Look at him," my mother said, sighing. "He looks like he's having the time of his life. If only I could do that," she added wistfully.

"You can," I told her.

She laughed. "Lea, I'm too old to learn how to surf."

"When you travel, test yourself. You'll never regret it," I said.

Mom sat up straight. "Wow, Lea, that sounds like something Ama would have said."

I nodded. "She wrote it in her travel journal."

As Mom gazed at the photo of the surfer, I typed in the caption, "Surfers young and old ride the waves in Brazil, but they all have one thing in common— the sheer joy of being one with the ocean."

"Thank you, Lea," Mom said, kissing the top of my head.

"For what?"

"For the nudge I needed."

The next day, while my mother went in search of surfing lessons, I came up with the idea for a hike.

"We can explore the cliffs—we haven't done that yet, and I can take photos," I explained.

"A hike?" Zac asked. "Just the two of us?"

"What about inviting your father?" Dad asked. "I've heard he's quite the explorer."

" . . . and Dad, too," I said, trying not to laugh.

"Well, I sort of thought I'd spend some time with Paloma," my brother informed me. "Don't you want to see Camila?"

"Camila's scared of heights, so she wouldn't like hiking up on the cliffs," I said. "Besides, what's wrong with spending time with me?"

"I've spent nearly every minute with you since you got here," Zac said. His voice softened. "But I only have one more day to spend with Paloma."

"That's true, but . . . " I trailed off. We *had* been around each other nonstop, yet somehow it felt as if we had hardly spent any time together. Almost as if

there had been an invisible wall between us. *If only I could prove to him that I'm not just a little kid anymore,* I thought to myself, *maybe he'd actually want to hang out with me.*

Just then, Dad stepped in front of us. "Ta da!" He was all decked out in his Amazon hiking gear, the vest with too many pockets, the complicated pants, the hat with flaps on the sides and back . . .

Zac and I moaned.

"Come on, kids," Dad said, grabbing some fruit bars and bottles of water and tucking them into his vest pockets. "I just need a moment to write a note to Mom, and then let's go on a hike!"

As Dad looked for a pen, Zac and I glanced at each other, not saying a word.

Finally Zac cleared his throat. "Say, Dad, I was thinking that maybe you two could go without me—"

"Nonsense!" my father said. "I haven't been hiking with my kids for years. Come on, Zac, get ready. Let's go!"

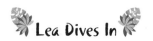

Hiking up the cliffs turned out to be a lot harder than any of us had imagined. The trail started off easy with lots of low inclines and flat sections, and then all of a sudden it got very steep as it zigged and zagged up the hill, and the foliage became thicker and denser. The paths were narrow and rocky, and every now and then I'd trip on a vine or slip on the loose gravel. Zac charged ahead, as if he was just trying to get the hike over with. Dad and I tried to keep up with him, but I stopped now and then to take photos. When I saw two brightly colored macaws perched in the nook of a twisty tree trunk, I stepped carefully off the trail to get a good shot.

"Can you get any slower?" Zac asked as I returned to the trail several yards behind him and Dad.

"What's your hurry?" I called back.

"Be nice, you two," Dad said. "Hey, take a look at this!" He pointed to a clearing. We followed him and found ourselves on a ledge looking over the ocean.

"What a view!" Dad said, pointing out over the cliff. "If it looks this great from this height, maybe we should go on the helicopter tour," he suggested. "I've

always wanted to ride in one."

The sea looked completely different from high up, and we could see deep down into it—the coral reefs, and even schools of fish. The boats sitting atop the clear water looked as if they were floating on air, and farther down the shore we saw surfers. I wondered if my mother was one of them. I hoped so.

I adjusted my hat to shield my eyes from the bright sun and slathered on more sunblock. Dad handed me a bottle of water and I took a big gulp. It was muggy up on the cliffs, but I wanted to climb higher. Maybe if we got a little farther away from town, we'd see some wildlife, like lizards and monkeys scampering up the trees! But Zac had already started heading back down the path in the direction we had come.

"Where are you going?" I called to him.

"It's too hot," he said. "I think we should head back."

"Just a little farther," I begged. "Please, Zac?"

"Whatever." My brother shrugged and turned around.

Trying to soften his mood, I quickly snapped

a picture of his grumpy face. I looked at the photo and giggled. "Paloma's going to love this one!"

"What?" he said, perking up. "No! Cricket, don't you dare." He lunged toward me but I made a quick escape, running up the path.

"Wait up, you two!" Dad called to us.

I ran ahead, jumping over fallen trees and ducking under leafy branches. After a while the path began to thin, and we seemed to be in an area that wasn't as well traveled. I stopped to take a picture of a braided-twisted tangle of vines that looked like a modern-art sculpture. Suddenly, Dad stepped into the shot. He pushed his hands and one foot through the vines and began to thrash about, shouting, "It's alive! It's a man-eating vine—run for your lives!"

Laughing, I clicked the camera, but before I could check to be sure I got the shot, Zac grabbed my arm, saying, "You heard Dad—run for your life! I'll race you to the top!" and I had no choice but to sprint after him. Still I managed to snap some pictures of Zac, who finally seemed to be having a good time. I got a good shot of him swinging like a monkey on the low branch of a tree with big hanging pods like

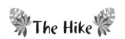

giant string beans, and a great action shot of him leaping off a rock formation that looked like a face.

Finally, laughing and panting, we stopped to wait for Dad.

When Dad caught up to us, he put his hands on his knees to catch his breath. "Let's have some water," he said. "Then I think we'd better head back."

"Aw, come on!" I replied, squinting through the trees. "It's like being in a jungle. Let's keep going!"

"It *is* a jungle," Zac said, picking a leaf out of my hair. "And I think we may have lost the path."

"What?" I looked around but saw only tall trees and dense undergrowth. Zac was right—we had completely lost the trail.

"Well, we're exploring, right?" I said brightly. "That's what exploring *means*: to forge ahead where no one else has been."

"That's what *getting lost* means," Zac countered.

"I'm making an executive decision," Dad said firmly, holding up both hands. "We're going back. Besides," he said, looking at his watch, "your mom should be done with her surfing lesson soon."

Zac scowled at me and followed Dad as he

pushed his way through the bushes. After hitting
a wall of brambles, we turned around. Yet we found
that going back was even harder than going forward. The underbrush was so thick in places that
it scraped my arms and legs. We weren't making
much progress.

"I think we're lost," I said finally.

Zac and Dad didn't seem to hear. They kept
pushing ahead.

"Um, excuse me?" I called to them.

"What?" Zac said sharply.

His tone surprised me, and I flinched. "We're
lost," I said quietly.

Zac looked irritated. "Don't you think we know
that?"

"Zac—" Dad warned. "Wait! I think I see . . . "
His voice trailed off as he pushed through some low
palm leaves. "Yes! Behold, the ocean!"

We stood several feet from the edge of the
cliff, and we could see the wide expanse of ocean
before us.

"I don't see the beach," Dad said, scratching his
chin. "We must be quite a ways farther along the cliff

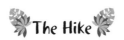

from where we stopped before. Zac, did you bring your phone?"

He shook his head. "I left it at the hotel."

"You left it at the hotel?" I exclaimed. "What were you thinking?"

"I was thinking that we'd just be taking a short walk. But then we went on this crazy hike. It's not my fault we're lost."

"All right, let's stay calm," Dad said.

Zac and I both snapped our mouths shut.

Dad took a deep breath and squinted past us. "We know where the ocean is, so we're not lost. It's just the trail that's lost," he said with a rueful smile. "But I think if we just follow the edge of the cliff—" He took a step forward, and the rocks beneath his feet shifted.

Before we knew what was happening, he had disappeared over the side of the cliff.

Action Shot
Chapter 14

Instinctively, I started toward the cliff's edge.
"Wait—stop!" Zac ordered, grabbing my arm.

"Dad! Dad!" I cried. I had never felt so scared
in my entire life. My hands trembled uncontrollably,
and my legs could barely hold me up.

Just then we heard it, the most glorious sound
I had ever heard—

"Owww!"

Dad was alive!

"Dad!" I called. "Are you okay?"

"Uh, not really," Dad said. "My sunglasses are
broken. Oh, and my leg, too."

I could tell that he was trying to make a joke, but
his voice sounded shaky.

Cautiously, Zac made his way toward the edge
and peered over the side. I inched forward, too,

116

keeping a good distance from the cliff's edge. I could see that Dad had landed on a rock ledge about ten feet below us.

He lay on his side, wincing as he tried to sit up. Then he shook his head at Zac. "I'm not going to be able to get back up there myself."

"I'll go for help," Zac called. "Lea will stay here with you."

"No!" Dad ordered. "You two stay together." He patted his vest. "I've got water and snacks, so I'll be fine." He gave us a brave smile, but he looked pale and small all alone on the rock ledge, with the vast ocean below.

"I can go faster without her," said Zac.

"Zac!" I yelled. "I'm not going to hold you back."

"Fine," he muttered. "Let's go."

"Dad," I called, "you're going to be okay, I promise."

"See?" Zac said, as he marched down a path. I had to run to keep up with him. "If you hadn't

made us go on this crazy hike ... "

What? He was blaming me?

"I didn't make you do anything," I told him.
"Besides, you're the one who went off the trail to
climb rocks."

Zac raised his eyebrows. "Oh, so now it's my
fault that Dad's in danger and we're hopelessly lost?
If you hadn't taken that picture of me—"

"What difference did *that* make?" I interrupted.
"And here I thought we were finally having fun, like
we used to ... "

We both fell silent as we continued trudging
through the trees. The trail, however, was nowhere
to be found.

"This way," Zac said, turning right around a
rotted tree stump.

"We just went that way. I recognize that stump.
Let's look over here." I pointed to a clearing ahead.

"We've been that way already," he snapped.
"It's a dead end."

"You don't know that," I shot back. "You just
refuse to do anything that isn't your idea."

"That's not the point," he argued. "Look, I know

what I'm doing. And you're just a kid."

I stopped in my tracks. So there it was. He had said what he thought of me: I was *just a kid*.

He opened his mouth to say something, and then seemed to think better of it and kept walking. Zac's words echoed in my head—*you're just a kid . . . you're just a kid*.

My eyes filled with tears. I was so worried about Dad. I wished Ama were here to wrap me in her arms and tell me everything was okay, just like that day I fell into the lake at Mark Twain State Park. I thought about what she had told me as she wiped my tears away. "You're capable of more than you know."

I closed my eyes and gripped Ama's compass, wishing it could help me now. But our problem wasn't knowing which direction to go in; our problem was finding a trail that could take us back down the cliff to civilization. And the compass couldn't help us with that.

Ahead of me, Zac was making his way around a rock formation. As I followed, something about the rock looked familiar. I squinted at it, and recognized the face I'd noticed when I had taken the

action shot of Zac leaping off it. I closed my eyes against the sting of tears.

How I wished we were back to that moment, all of us laughing and getting along—

My eyes flashed open. I did have a way to go back to that moment.

"Hey, Zac, I think I might know how to find our way out of here," I called.

"Oh yeah?" Zac stopped. "What's your brilliant idea?"

Ignoring his sarcasm, I held up my camera.

"Yes, I see you have a camera," Zac said, throwing his hands up. "Cricket, this is no time for jokes."

"Listen to me," I said urgently. "This can show us the way." Zac frowned skeptically, but I could tell he was curious. "Look—that's the rock you jumped from," I said, pointing.

"How can you be sure?" Zac asked.

"Because I can see it right here!" I held up my camera to show him. "I've been taking photos our entire hike. All we have to do is look at the photos and find the landmarks in them, and we can back-track our way down until we're back on the trail.

Action Shot

Look here," I said, pointing at a bush up ahead.
"That's where I took this picture." I showed him the
photo I'd taken of a bush with bright red flowers.

Zac's face softened. He shook his head in disbe-
lief. "Okay, we'll give it a try. Lead on, Captain."

At least he wasn't calling me Cricket. Together,
we found the tree with hanging pods that Zac had
swung from like a monkey, and then the tangle of
vines where Dad had pretended to be trapped, and
finally the spot overlooking the ocean where we had
stopped with Dad just an hour earlier. From there
we were able to find the path and follow it back to
the beach.

We jogged down the shore until we reached
Paloma's beach shack. It was very hot and we should
have been exhausted, but our bodies were running
on adrenaline. In the distance I could see Camila
helping Paloma organize the snorkel gear. We
shouted and ran toward them.

Zac spoke quickly in Portuguese, and Paloma
ran into the beach shack to get her cell phone and
started making calls. Within ten minutes, a rescue
team had mobilized.

"We need to find my mother," I told Paloma. "She was taking a surfing lesson at the beach near our hotel."

"Then I know where she is," Paloma said. "You go with Zac. I will find her."

"Lea can take us to our father," Zac announced to the rescue team first in English, then in Portuguese. He turned to me and we locked eyes. "You lead. We'll follow."

I touched Ama's compass. "Okay, everyone— let's go."

There was no time to be tired or scared as we hiked back up the trail. Camila and Zac stayed with me stride for stride, followed by the rescue workers. No one spoke. We were all focused on getting to Dad. Even after the main trail petered out, it wasn't hard to see where Dad, Zac, and I had walked—we had sort of made a temporary trail of bent grass and broken branches. And I recognized most of the landmarks without even checking my camera.

At last, Zac pushed the brush away and we were

at the precipice of the cliff. I looked down at the
ledge. My father looked pretty beat up and tired, but
his eyes lit up when he saw me.

"Dad!" I called. "Dad, help is here!"

"Thank goodness," he said, waving weakly to
the group standing behind me.

I was too relieved to cry or laugh, so instead
I hugged my brother, and he hugged me back. We
kept our arms around each other as the rescue team
rappelled down to my father.

Despite his pain, Dad kept the mood light, telling the rescuers things like "My kids were ignoring
me, so I thought I'd do something dramatic to get
their attention."

I laughed loudly. Never had his dumb jokes
seemed so hysterically funny.

Once the rescue workers reached my father, they
realized it was far too dangerous for them to even
attempt to carry him off the ledge and then down the
cliff, so they radioed for help.

Meanwhile, I watched as the medics set Dad's
leg in a temporary splint.

"Is it broken?" I called down.

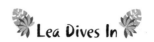
"Spectacularly broken!" Dad yelled back.

We could hear the helicopter before we could see it. It circled above us just like in the movies— only instead of a medical helicopter, it was the tour helicopter! I took photos as the helicopter hovered and a harness was lowered on a rope to the ledge where my father was now sitting up. One of the rescue workers secured the harness around Dad, and then slowly he was raised into the helicopter. Camila explained that the local police and rescue teams used the tourist helicopter for emergencies like this one.

I raised my camera and snapped one last shot. Dad was finally getting his helicopter ride, and I was sure he'd want a souvenir photo.

The rescue workers took us on a faster route back down, since they knew the terrain and the shortcuts. Camila stayed close to my side the entire way, gripping my arm.

"It means a lot to me that you would come up to the cliffs to help us," I said, squeezing her hand. "I know how you feel about heights. Obrigada."

"Our friendship is stronger than my fear of heights," Camila said. "Hey!" She held up our linked

hands and pointed to my wrist. "It's gone!"

"What's gone?" I asked, confused.

"Your wish bracelet," she said.

Sure enough, it had fallen off.

I met Camila's eyes. She smiled.

"Orange, right?" she asked.

I nodded and smiled back. "For courage."

Paloma met us on the path. Dad was already at a local hospital, and Mom was meeting him there. Senhora Cavalcante offered to drive us.

"Mom!" I cried, when I saw her in the waiting room. Zac and I both ran up and hugged her.

"How's Dad?" Zac asked.

"He's got a serious broken leg, and the doctors say that it's a miracle nothing else is broken. But he's going to be all right. I need to go give them some information," Mom said, motioning to the reception desk. "You two are my heroes."

Suddenly the weight of all that had happened hit me. I began to cry so hard that my shoulders shook and I couldn't talk. Zac took me in his arms, and I

buried my face in his shoulder as he hugged me.

"You were amazing," my brother said. "Dad's going to be okay because of your quick thinking. I should have had more faith in you. If there's ever anything I can do to make it up to you, Cricket, just ask."

We hugged for another minute or so; then I wiped away my tears on his shirt. "Well," I said, "there is one thing."

Zac got very serious. "What? Tell me. Anything."

I looked him straight in the eyes and said, "You can stop calling me Cricket."

He squinted in confusion. "But why? I've been calling you that ever since you were little. You used to love it!" He tried ruffling my hair, but I pulled away.

"Zac!" I said, my voice weary. "I'm not a little girl anymore, but you still treat me like one."

He paused and then cracked a smile. "C'mon, we're just having fun—"

I shook my head. "You don't take me seriously." Tears started to well in my eyes. I tried to blink them back. "You act like it's a pain to hang out with me.

I've waited months and months, and thought about you every day, Zac. I couldn't wait to see you. And now you act like it's no big deal that I'm here with you, and you'd rather be doing something else."

Despite every effort not to, I began to cry again. And I couldn't believe what happened next.

Zac's eyes teared up. My big brother was crying.

"You're wrong about not wanting to see you," he said in a shaky voice. "I've been looking forward to seeing you and Mom and Dad, so much. I love it here, but ever since Ama died, it's been really hard to be so far away here in Brazil, when everyone I love is back home in St. Louis. I even considered cutting my year short and leaving Brazil early, I was so homesick."

I stood stunned, not knowing what to do or say. I had never known Zac to be anything but super self-confident. I had no idea that he had been so homesick.

"I'm really sorry I got crabby and impatient with you," Zac went on. "I guess you're right—I do think of you as being the age you were when I left for college." He shook his head. "You're not seven anymore. I see that now."

I nodded, my heart too full to speak.

"You're strong and brave and smart. I'm really proud of you, Cricket."

"Lea," I corrected him with a smile.

"Right: Lea," Zac said, as if he were trying it on for size. "Honored to meet you, Lea," he said, sticking out his hand for a handshake. "I've heard great things about you."

Someplace Magical
Chapter 15

By the next day, everybody in the town of Praia Tropical was talking about the tourist who fell off the cliff and had to be rescued by helicopter. My father was famous—and so were my brother and I.

Everywhere we went, people shook our hands and asked Zac to share details. He retold the story so often that he began to embellish it, each time adding more drama and chaos. Even though he spoke in Portuguese, I could tell what Zac was saying by his wild gestures. But one thing remained consistent every time he told the story—he always said that it was his sister who had saved the day. *"Minha irmã é minha heroína,"* he'd say, throwing his arm around my shoulders. *My sister is my hero.* I always blushed with embarrassment, but I must admit it made me feel good inside.

What didn't make me feel good was that Dad was still in the hospital. Although his leg didn't require surgery, it was badly broken. Mom stayed with him, and encouraged Zac and me to go out and enjoy our last day at the beach.

"I have a surprise for you," Zac told me as we walked barefoot along the shore.

"A surprise?" I asked.

Zac grinned and broke into a jog, waving over his shoulder. "C'mon!"

I ran after him, and soon we were racing each other, sprinting over the sand and making splashes in the warm water that washed onto shore.

I felt a rush of happiness. Things were finally back to normal between us—but it was a new normal. We had talked into the night, but it wasn't like before, when I'd tell him things and he'd give me advice. It was more like a great conversation between friends. We talked about Zac's host family in the rainforest, and I shared Ama's travel journals. Together we looked at photos of our grandmother's travels in Australia. *I always make it a point to befriend the locals,* Ama had written. *They know all the best secret places to visit!*

"Good advice, isn't it, Zac?" I said. "After all, what if we hadn't met Camila—and Paloma?" I added, giving him a nudge and grinning when he blushed.

By the time we neared Paloma's beach shack, we were both out of breath and laughing. Paloma and Camila were lounging in the hammock, and waved hello as we approached.

"Are you ready?" Camila asked. She pointed to a beat-up red wooden boat tied to a stake in the sand and bobbing gently in the blue Bahia sea.

"Ready for what?" I asked.

I could hardly contain my excitement as Zac, Camila, and Paloma led me to the boat. Inside was a basket filled with cold drinks, *cocadas*, the chewy shredded coconut candy that I had grown to love, and *coxinha*, Zac's favorite minced chicken croquettes.

Zac and Paloma whispered to each other as Camila looked on, smiling.

"Where are we going?" I asked as Zac held the boat steady so that Camila and I could climb in.

"To see something you've never seen before," Camila replied. Her eyes were smiling. "That's all I'm going to tell you."

Lea Dives In

It took Paloma a couple of tries to start the ancient outboard motor, and then we were off. Our boat left a ribbon of white foam in its wake.

The boat began to slow as we neared a rocky bank surrounded by coconut palms with thick trunks. It looked like paradise. The warm sun blanketed us as a light breeze blew and the palm trees swayed lazily. I could hear the call of the seagulls, but what was really beckoning me was the water.

Paloma cut the engine and anchored near the shore as Zac passed out the snorkel gear that was piled in the boat.

"Here, Lea," Zac said, handing me my mask.

"Obrigada," I replied. I took off my compass necklace and handed it to Paloma. She knew how special it was to me and how I didn't want anything to happen to it. She tucked the necklace away in the cooler for safekeeping.

By then I was practically an expert and slipped on my mask and snorkel without hesitation. I looked out at the ocean. A few days ago the water had made me nervous, and now here I was, eager to explore what was below its surface. With the fins firmly on my feet, I picked up my camera and jumped off the boat and into the ocean.

As I slowly submerged my head into the water, I relished the sudden silence, punctuated only by the sound of me breathing through the snorkel. I sounded like Darth Vader, only I bet that he never got to go snorkeling! I looked around and swam, taking pictures of the coral where the reefs came up near the surface. It was like a whole new world, like outer space, only here on earth. I felt like an explorer.

Paloma swam up to me, with Zac and Camila close behind, and motioned for me to follow her. The sun illuminated the ocean, casting a golden glow through the water. Bright green plants gently swayed as a school of silver fish darted past, and colorful coral walls rose and fell like a roller coaster. Then we rounded a bend, and my breath caught in my throat.

It was a shipwreck—a real shipwreck!

It looked like something out of a pirate movie. It was about the length of two school buses and had lodged itself just beneath the surface of the water on a coral reef. I swam faster, my camera leading the way. If I didn't take pictures, no one at home

would believe me! At first, I thought the ship looked strangely fuzzy, but upon closer inspection I could see that barnacles and moss had grown on its surface. Fish swam in and out of the portholes. I took photo after photo, until Paloma motioned for all of us to surface.

"Amazing," Zac said. "Lea, are you getting pictures of this?"

I held up my camera. "It's all here," I said. I couldn't wait to post photos to my blog and tell my class back home all about seeing the shipwreck!

"You can swim around, but not inside," Paloma reminded us.

I gave Paloma a thumbs-up, and then swam over to the other side of the wreck. A school of bright yellow fish swam slowly past, and as I began taking shots, a giant sea turtle suddenly appeared in my view, gliding majestically through the sunlit water. It was almost as big as I was. I gasped with excitement—wondering if I should try to follow it, fumbling as salt water seeped into my mouthpiece, and then—*I dropped my camera.*

I reached for it, but it was already below my feet.

134

🌺 Someplace Magical 🌺

My heart turned over as I watched my camera—my camera from Ama with all my Brazil photos on it—fall slowly through the water and out of my reach. A cloud of small fish darted away from a pile of rusted chain where they had been hiding as my camera came to rest on the hull of the ship.

I began to chide myself. The camera had a cord for my wrist—why hadn't I used it? If I had, it wouldn't have slipped from my hands. In my haste to get into the water, I had completely forgotten about it.

I lifted my head out of the water and could see Camila's and Paloma's snorkels bobbing up and down as they swam on the other side of the ship.

Zac waved to me. "Everything okay, Lea?" he called out.

As I treaded water, I was about to ask him for help, but stopped. This was something I needed to do myself. I waved back, and then I took a big gulp of air and dove toward the ship's hull.

I remembered what Paloma had taught me and blew air through my snorkel as I sank deeper, sending a stream of bubbles above me. My camera was

135

in clear sight. But before I could get to it, my lungs began to burn—my breath was running out. In a panic, I used my fins to propel me back to the top, amazed by how quickly I could swim with them when I needed to.

When I got to the surface, my snorkel was filled with water. I spit it out of my mouth, gasping for air. Then I turned over, panting and shaken, and floated on my back to take a rest.

I had never tried snorkeling underwater, and I hadn't been sure I would be able to. As I floated, I thought again of the turtle. It was so graceful and at home in the water—yet at one time it had been a hatchling, struggling to make its way across the sand. Against all odds, it had not only made it to the sea, it had survived and grown to become the awe-inspiring creature I had seen.

I took another deep breath and dove down to the bottom, determined not to surface without my camera. But once more, I came up empty-handed. Again I rested, and again I tried, this time getting closer. Finally, I filled my lungs with air and swam down slowly and steadily using long, strong strokes.

My fingertips touched the camera—and then with a sure hand, I grasped it tightly and propelled myself upward.

When I broke through to the surface, squinting in the bright sunlight, I saw my brother grinning at me. Had he been watching the whole time?

"Lea to the rescue!" he called to me. "Ama would have been proud."

I grinned and gave him a thumbs-up before slipping the camera's strap around my wrist.

The Gift

Chapter 16

It was our last morning in Praia Tropical. Zac had gone off to spend a little more time with Paloma while Mom, Dad, and I ate breakfast at the hotel's quaint coffee shop overlooking the ocean. I was excited to visit Zac's host family in the rainforest, but sad that I would have to say good-bye to Camila— and the ocean. That's when I remembered that the Queen of the Sea festival was today.

"So, what time are we leaving?" I asked, keeping my fingers crossed that there would be time to go to the festival with Camila.

Mom and Dad shared a look and then turned to me. "Actually," Mom said, "your father and I have been talking. And we've decided that it would be too difficult for us to go to the rainforest."

My face fell. "You mean our vacation is over?"

"No," said Dad. "*You're* still going to the rainforest. Your mom and I will stay here in Praia Tropical."

"What do you mean?" I asked. "Is this because of Dad's leg?"

Mom nodded and pointed to Dad's full-leg cast. "The leg is badly broken, which will make traveling around the rainforest very difficult."

I felt terrible. After all, exploring the cliffs had been my idea. I started to apologize, but Dad interrupted me. "Lea, I wanted to go hiking and exploring as much as you did. And if it weren't for your smart thinking, I might still be out there on that ledge."

Mom nodded. "Zac sat down with us this morning and told us everything. And when we told him that we were thinking about cutting our trip short, he convinced us to let you go alone with him to the rainforest while your father heals and gets used to walking with crutches here in Praia Tropical."

"He did?" I could hardly believe it. "Zac, my brother?"

Dad smiled. "Yes, that Zac. He said you were old enough."

Mom looked serious, though. "We've all noticed how brave you've become." She reached across the table and squeezed my hand, her eyes misty. "Didn't I tell you that you have Ama's spark? You just had to find it within yourself. What did she always say? *'Travel and test—'"*

"When you travel, test yourself. You'll never regret it." I smiled. "Mom, you tested yourself, too," I reminded her. "You went surfing!"

"That I did," my mother said. "And do you know who inspired me?"

I shook my head.

"You!" she said.

Dad raised his glass of orange juice. "To Lea— and Ama!"

"To Ama!" Mom and I chimed in.

My grandmother was right. I had tested my- self—and I had no regrets.

Soon after we finished breakfast, Zac returned

to the hotel. "We'd better hurry if we want to get to the Queen of the Sea festival before we leave for the airport," he said, giving me a wink. He must have known that Mom and Dad had just told me that he and I would be going on our own to the rainforest. "Come on, Paloma and Camila are waiting for us at Moda Praia."

I grinned and picked up my camera.

As Zac and I walked toward town, celebration was everywhere. Musicians lined the streets, their melodies and rhythms filling the air as festivalgoers made their way toward the statue. Zac and I were both deep in thought. Just a few days ago we might have been joking, or fighting, or getting on each other's nerves. But this morning, we walked together in contented silence.

When we arrived at the store, Camila hurried up to me. She was wearing the colorful dress I had first seen in her store. I had been so busy that I had almost forgotten about it. I glanced around the store and saw that they had sold out of the dresses. I was disappointed, but reminded myself that it was just a dress and that I had something even better to take

home with me: my memories of my trip to Praia Tropical—and all of my photos, too.

"We should go," Paloma said. "The festival has already started."

"Wait," Camila said, running behind the counter to grab a package. "This is for you, Lea." She handed me a Moda Praia box tied with an orange ribbon. "Open it!"

I undid the bow, and my heart leaped when I saw what was inside—the dress! I threw my arms around Camila, and thanked her and Senhora Cavalcante.

"Try it on!" Paloma said, pulling back the curtain to the dressing room.

I grinned and stepped inside before Paloma pulled the curtain closed. I quickly slipped on the dress and looked in the mirror. As I admired the cheerful colors, I felt a wave of joy rush through me. I centered Ama's compass over my heart and opened the curtain.

"It fits you perfectly!" Camila said, clapping.

I gave a curtsy as Zac and Paloma joined in the applause. Then I thanked Senhora Cavalcante once more, and followed the group outside.

The Gift

The cobblestone streets were already crowded with families, couples, tourists, and locals. The small town had swelled with all the people who had come to pay homage to the Queen of the Sea. Food carts sold light-colored sweets to match Yemanjá's white dress, such as honeyed rice and sweet corn pudding. Camila and I shared a sweet coconut milk jelly called *manjar branco*, while Zac and Paloma munched on puffed rice. Most people were wearing all white or a light blue—Yemanjá's colors, Camila told me, adjusting the white and blue flowers in her arms that she had brought as a gift for Yemanjá. That's when I realized that I had completely forgotten to bring a gift for the Queen of the Sea.

We finally arrived at the mermaid statue. Revelers danced to the beat of the drums and laid their offerings at the base of the shrine, which glistened as the sun reflected in the shards of blue tiles. I looked up at the Queen of the Sea, reigning over the crowd with her long flowing hair and serene presence. She was the loveliest mermaid I could imagine. Paloma had brought her a small bottle of perfume. How I wished I had brought

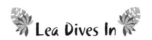

something worthy of her to give.

"Come dance!" Paloma shouted over the sounds of the festival as she and Camila started moving to the beat. They held out their hands to us.

Zac and I looked at each other. Neither of us was very good at dancing. But the energy of the music was infectious, and before we knew it, the girl and boy from St. Louis, Missouri, were dancing along with the people of Bahia, paying homage to the Queen of the Sea.

I bounced up and down, doing my awkward version of dancing. Some of the kids at school say that I dance like a kangaroo. But I was having so much fun I didn't care.

I shouted over the music, "Camila, the next time you visit your relatives in Chicago, you should come see me in St. Louis!"

"Is Chicago far from St. Louis?" she asked.

"Not really. It's just down the road about three hundred miles. It's practically next door!"

"Maybe I could come, then," Camila said. "I'll ask my parents." She reached into her pocket and pulled out two bright pink ribbons. "For friendship,"

she said as she tied one around my wrist with three knots, while I made a wish for Camila to visit me in St. Louis. Then Camila extended her arm toward me. "Now, you tie one on my wrist," she said.

"Um, dois, três," I said, counting in Portuguese as I tied each knot.

All of a sudden a loud bell rang, and the crowd cheered.

"What does that mean?" I asked Camila.

"I'll show you," she shouted. "Come with me!"

Zac, Paloma, and I followed her down to the sandy shore. Boats were lined up in a row as if standing at attention and waiting for their orders. Camila pointed at a line of fishermen carrying baskets overflowing with gifts. "They will deliver these offerings to Yemanjá," she explained. "Remember, if the baskets and gifts sink, it means that she has accepted them—and in return, she promises good luck for the coming year."

If only Ama were with me, I thought as I ran my finger around the face of the compass. *She would have thought to bring something special for Yemanjá. But what offering could I give?*

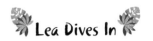 Lea Dives In

As the first boats headed out to sea, I could hear my grandmother saying, "Lea, when you visit a place, you don't just take—you leave something behind."

"Wait, stop. *Pare!*" I shouted, waving at the fishermen. *"Pare!* Stop!" I ran toward the water and kicked off my shoes.

"Lea, where are you going?" Zac shouted.

"Lea!" Camila cried. "Come back!"

I splashed into the water, chasing after a fisherman with leathery skin and kind eyes. He had just lifted his basket of gifts onto his boat and was about to set sail.

"Are you crazy?" Zac called to me over the water. "What's going on?"

"Don't worry," I called back. "I won't be long." I tugged on the fisherman's shirt. He turned with a confused look on his face.

In that moment, it seemed as if the sound of the music and chatter from the crowds stopped—and the ocean had never looked so beautiful. Slowly, I lifted Ama's compass necklace from around my neck.

"For Yemanjá," I said, motioning to the statue

 # The Gift

on the shore. "This is for her." I took one last look at
the compass, kissed it, and then gently placed it in
his basket.

The fisherman nodded solemnly.

"Obrigada," I said, smiling at him. And suddenly it was as if the volume came back on. Cheers filled
the air as the boats set sail.

My face was wet, and I realized that tears were
streaming down my cheeks.

I felt someone place a hand on my shoulder. It
was Zac, who had waded into the water. He didn't say
anything. He didn't have to. Instead, we stood side by
side and watched the last boat head out to sea.

Glossary of Portuguese Words

NOTE: In the pronunciation guide below, you'll sometimes see a small *m* or *n* at the end of a syllable. In these places, pronounce the letter very gently or don't quite finish saying it. In Brazil, an *l* at the end of a word is often pronounced "oo."

açaí *(ah-sah-EE)*—a small, dark-purple fruit harvested from the açaí palm tree, which is native to Brazil

água de coco *(AH-gwah juh CO-co)*—coconut water

amanhã *(ah-mahn-YAH^n)*—tomorrow

amiga *(ah-MEE-guh)*—female friend

Amigos do Oceano Santuário das Tartarugas Marinhas *(ah-MEE-gooss doo o-say-AH-noo sahn-too-AH-ree-oo dass tar-tuh-ROO-gahss mah-REE^n-yahss)*—Friends of the Ocean Sea Turtle Sanctuary

Bahia *(bah-EE-uh)*—one of Brazil's twenty-six states, located on the eastern side of the country on the Atlantic coast; the birthplace of Brazil

Baianas *(bah-ee-AH-nahss)*—women of Bahia who dress in white to honor the Afro Brazilian religion of Candomblé

Brasil *(brah-ZEE-oo)*—Brazil

capoeira *(kah-po-AY-ruh)*—a Brazilian martial art that combines dance, acrobatics, and music

castelo de areia *(kah-STEH-loo juh uh-REE-yuh)*—sand castle

Claro que sim. *(KLAH-roo keh SEE^m)*—Yes, of course.

cocadas *(ko-KAH-duhss)*—Brazilian coconut candy

coxinha *(KO-shee^n-yuh)*—a fried, drumstick-shaped Brazilian snack stuffed with a creamy chicken filling

Estes são meus amigos. *(EHSS-tehss saoo MEH-ooz uh-MEE-gooss)*—These are my friends.

família *(fah-MEE-lee-uh)*—family

mãe *(maee)*—mother

manjar branco *(mah-JAH-huh BRAHN-koo)*—Brazilian coconut pudding

meu nome é *(MEH-oo NO-may EH)*—my name is

Minha irmã é minha heroína. *(MEE^n-yuh eer-MAH^n eh MEE^n-yuh ay-ro-EE-nuh)*—My sister is my heroine.

Moda Praia *(MO-duh PRAH-yuh)*—beach fashion

moqueca *(mo-KEH-kuh)*—a Brazilian seafood stew made with coconut milk, red palm oil, tomato, onions, garlic, and coriander

obrigada *(o-bree-GAH-duh)*—thank you (spoken by females)

obrigado *(o-bree-GAH-doo)*—thank you (spoken by males)

oi *(oy)*—hi

olá *(o-LAH)*—hello

orixá *(o-ree-SHAH)*—a god or spirit from African religious traditions recognized in Brazil

pão francês *(pahw frahn-SAYSS)*—French bread

pare *(PAH-ray)*—stop

por favor *(por fah-VOR)*—please

pastel de forno *(pah-STEHL juh FOR-noo)*—savory hand pie with a flaky crust stuffed with various fillings such as cheese or meat

Pelourinho *(peh-lo-oo-REE^{n}-yoo)*—the historic district of Salvador, Bahia

praia *(PRAH-yuh)*—beach

real *(ray-AHL)*—unit of Brazilian currency

saltenha *(sahl-TEHN-yuh)*—savory pastry with sweet and spicy meat filling

Salvador *(sahl-vuh-DOR)*—the capital city of Bahia

Senhor do Bonfim *(seh[n]-YOR doo BOH[n]-fee[m])*—the savior of Bahia who guards the city, grants wishes, and provides miracles

Senhora *(seh[n]-YO-ruh)*—Mrs.

um, dois, três *(oo[m] doyss trayss)*—one, two, three

Você está visitando? *(vo-SEH eh-STAH vee-see-TAH[n]-doo)*—Are you visiting?

Yemanjá *(yeh-mah[n]-ZHAH)*—One of the orixás from African religious traditions, Bahia's Queen of the Ocean is honored with a festival on February 2

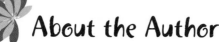

About the Author

Lisa Yee has written over a dozen books for young people. She loves to research and was thrilled when Lea's stories took her to the Bahia coast of Brazil. There, she snorkeled among the coral reefs, sampled local foods, and learned about the traditions and customs of the region. Lisa also visited the Amazon rainforest, where she fished for piranha, swam in the Amazon River, and even ate roasted larvae during a hike through the rainforest. However, the highlights of her travels were meeting an alligator, a boa constrictor, and a baby sloth—though not all at once!

You can learn more about Lisa at www.lisayee.com and see photos of her Brazilian adventures.